a bag of marbles

Based on the memoir by **JOSEPH JOFFO**

Adapted by **KRIS**

Illustrated by **VINCENT BAILLY**

Translated by **EDWARD GAUVIN**

DISCARDED

GRAPHIC UNIVERSE™ • MINNEAPOLIS

For us. All of us.

Dedicated to all those who know why they fought,

and those still fighting today.

—K. and V.B.

Happy as God in France.

—Yiddish proverb

First American edition published in 2013 by Graphic Universe™.
Published by arrangement with Futuropolis.

Copyright © by Futuropolis 2011 and 2012
English translation Copyright © 2013 by Lerner Publishing Group, Inc.

Graphic Universe™ is a trademark of Lerner Publishing Group, Inc.

Graphic Universe™
A division of Lerner Publishing Group, Inc.
241 First Avenue North
Minneapolis, MN 55401 U.S.A.

Website address: www.lernerbooks.com

Main body text set in Andy
Typeface provided by Monotype Typography

Library of Congress Cataloging-in-Publication Data

Kris, 1972–
  [Sac de billes. English]
  A bag of marbles : the graphic novel / based on the novel by Joseph Joffo ; adapted by Kris ; illustrated by Vincent Bailly ; translated by Edward Gauvin.
     p. cm
  Summary: In 1941, ten-year-old Joseph Joffo and his older brother, Maurice, must hide their Jewish heritage and undertake a long and dangerous journey from Nazi-occupied Paris to reach their other brothers in the free zone.
  ISBN 978–1–4677–0700–8 (lib. bdg. : alk. paper)
  ISBN 978–1–4677–1651–2 (eBook)
  1. Joffo, Joseph—Juvenile fiction. 2. Joffo, Maurice—Juvenile fiction. 3. Holocaust, Jewish (1939–1945)—France—Juvenile fiction. 4. Graphic novels. [1. Graphic novels. 2. Joffo, Joseph—Fiction. 3. Joffo, Maurice—Fiction. 4. Holocaust, Jewish (1939–1945)—France—Fiction. 5. Jews—France—Fiction. 6. World War, 1939–1945—France—Fiction. 7. France—History—German occupation, 1940–1945—Fiction.] I. Bailly, Vincent, illustrator. II. Gauvin, Edward. III. Joffo, Joseph. Sac de billes. IV. Title.
PZ7.7.K74Bag 2013
741.5'944—dc23 [B]   2013002284

Manufactured in the United States of America
1 – DP – 7/15/13

ÉTES-VOUS
PLUS FRANCAIS
QUE LUI?

POPULATIONS
abandonnées,

faites confiance
AU SOLDAT ALLEMAND

33°

part one

C'MON, JO, WILL
YOU GO ALREADY?

WHAT THE HECK'S
TAKING YOU SO
LONG?

I'M NOT.

WHEN YOU LOOK AWAY LIKE THAT I CAN ALWAYS TELL YOU'RE BLUBBERING.

HERE, TAKE IT.

TEN-YEAR-OLDS DON'T CRY OVER MARBLES.

WE BETTER HURRY. WE WERE SUPPOSED TO BE HOME HALF AN HOUR AGO! WE'RE GONNA GET IT!

DING

JO, MAURICE! MY LITTLE HOOLIGANS, HOME AT LAST.

HOMEWORK! HOP TO IT! YOUR MOTHER'S GOING TO HAVE A FIT.

7

YOU DONE YET?

HOLD YOUR HORSES! WE'VE BEEN AT IT LESS THAN A MINUTE. IF WE DON'T DRAG IT OUT A LITTLE, MAMA WILL JUST SEND US BACK HERE.

OK, THAT SHOULD BE LONG ENOUGH. LET'S GO!

DONE ALREADY?

EASIER THAN A BUZZ CUT, RIGHT, ALBERT?

WHERE TO?

DO SOME DOORBELL DITCHES? HEAD DOWN TO THE CANAL?

SS...

YOU THINK THEY NEED A HAIRCUT?

HIER, WARUM NICHT? *

JA, ES SIEHT MIR GUT AUS. AUF GEHT'S! **

DING

Jüdisches Geschäft**

* JEWISH BUSINESS

* WHY NOT HERE?
** SURE LOOKS GOOD TO ME. LET'S GO!

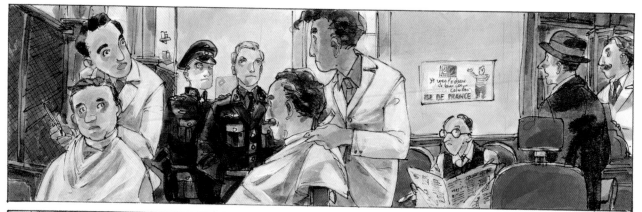

IF WHOEVER'S NEXT WOULD PLEASE HAVE A SEAT...

YES. AND PARTED TO THE RIGHT, PLEASE.

THANKS.

WOULD YOU LIKE IT SHORT?

* THE MAN KNOWS KARLSRUHE! HE IS FROM ALSACE!

ARE THOSE YOUR BOYS?

YES. THEY'RE LITTLE HOODLUMS.

THE WAR IS ROTTEN. THE JEWS ARE TO BLAME.

YOU THINK SO?

I'M SURE OF IT.

VOILÀ!

THERE YOU ARE. ALL DONE.

VERY GOOD. THANKS!

YOU'RE HAPPY WITH YOUR HAIRCUTS?

VERY GOOD. EXCELLENT.

BEFORE YOU GO, I SHOULD TELL YOU THIS. ALL THESE PEOPLE HERE ARE JEWS.

I WAS TALKING ABOUT RICH JEWS.

NOW, WHERE WERE WE?

THE ADVENTURES OF YOUR GRANDFATHER, JACOB JOFFO.

WHERE DID I LEAVE OFF?

THE POGROMS WERE STARTING!

AH, YES.

THE POGROMS WERE STARTING.

ALL THIS HAPPENED LONG AGO, IN THE RUSSIAN PART OF BESSARABIA...

OF ALL OUR CHILDHOOD MEMORIES— MAURICE'S AND MINE—THESE FAMILY STORY NIGHTS WERE AMONG THE BEST.

MY GRANDFATHER'S ADVENTURES, INTERLOCKED LIKE NESTING DOLLS, WERE SET AGAINST A BACKDROP OF DESERTS WHITE WITH SNOW AND TWISTING ALLEYWAYS IN TOWNS STREWN WITH GILDED CUPOLAS.

HE HAD TWELVE SONS. HE WAS RICH, GENEROUS, HAPPY, AND RESPECTED IN HIS VILLAGE SOUTH OF ODESSA . . . UNTIL THE DAY THE POGROMS BEGAN.

I ENVISIONED BRANDISHED RIFLE BUTTS AND FLEEING PEASANTS. BEFORE MY EYES PLAYED WHIRLWINDS OF FLAME AND SABER BLADES, AND TOWERING OVER IT ALL WAS THE COLOSSAL FIGURE OF MY GRANDFATHER.

AT NIGHT, DISGUISED AS A PEASANT AND WITH THE CLEAR CONSCIENCE OF A RIGHTEOUS MAN WHO WON'T STAND BY WHILE HIS FRIENDS ARE KILLED, HE WOULD BEAT UP SOLDIERS. THEN HE'D HEAD HOME, WHISTLING A YIDDISH TUNE.

BUT THEN THE MASSACRES GOT WORSE. MY GRANDFATHER UNDERSTOOD THAT ALL BY HIMSELF HE COULD NOT KNOCK OUT THE THREE BATTALIONS THAT THE CZAR HAD SENT TO THE AREA. THE WHOLE FAMILY HAD TO FLEE—AND FAST.

WHAT FOLLOWED WAS A LIVELY AND PICTURESQUE PROGRESSION ACROSS ALL OF EUROPE, FULL OF STORMY NIGHTS, REVELRY, LAUGHTER, TEARS, AND DEATH.

AND THEN ONE DAY, THEY CROSSED THE LAST BORDER. THERE WERE FIELDS OF WHEAT, SINGING BIRDS, AND BRIGHT VILLAGES WITH RED ROOFTOPS AND A STEEPLE.

ON THE BIGGEST HOUSE WAS AN INSCRIPTION: *LIBERTÉ, ÉGALITÉ, FRATERNITÉ.* THEN FEAR LEFT THE REFUGEES, FOR THEY KNEW THEY HAD ARRIVED.

IN FRANCE.

AH . . . IF YOUR MOTHER'S HERE, IT MUST MEAN IT'S PAST YOUR BEDTIME. OFF TO SLEEP!

THAT NIGHT WE LISTENED AS WE USUALLY DID: RIVETED, MOUTHS WIDE OPEN.

THE LOVE THE FRENCH PEOPLE HAVE FOR THEIR COUNTRY COMES SO NATURALLY. BUT I KNOW OF NO ONE WHO EVER LOVED THAT COUNTRY AS MUCH AS MY PARENTS, WHO WERE BORN FIVE THOUSAND MILES AWAY.

NOT YET. I WAS JUST WONDERING . . .

YOU . . . YOU DON'T THINK THERE'LL BE TROUBLE NOW THAT THE GERMANS ARE HERE?

SO LONG AS THE WORDS *LIBERTÉ, ÉGALITÉ, FRATERNITÉ* ARE WRITTEN ON OUR TOWN HALLS, WE'LL BE ALL RIGHT HERE.

NO, NOT HERE. NOT IN FRANCE. NEVER.

GOOD NIGHT, CHILDREN.

GOOD NIGHT . . .

* JEW

HEY, FELLAS! GET A LOAD OF JOFFO!

YOU'RE NOT THE ONLY ONE. SOME OLDER KIDS GOT THEM TOO.

HEY, YOU A KIKE?

IT'S ON ACCOUNT OF THE KIKES THERE'S A WAR ON.

YOU'RE A REAL MORON! YOU THINK THIS WAR'S ALL JO'S FAULT?

SURE DO! WE GOTTA GET RID OF ALL THE YIDS!

YOU SEE THE NOSE ON HIM?

WHAT'S WRONG WITH MY NOSE? IT'S THE SAME AS IT WAS YESTERDAY!

IN LINE, CHILDREN! SINGLE FILE!

CLOSE YOUR NOTEBOOKS NOW. AGAIN, FROM MEMORY: THE RHÔNE VALLEY...

THE RHÔNE VALLEY DIVIDES THE ANCIENT MOUNTAIN MASSES OF THE MASSIF CENTRAL FROM—

Di, DiLiNG

C'MON, JO, HURRY UP! RECESS!

HEY, KIKE!

HEY, KIKE! KIKE!

KIKE! KIKE!

KIKE!

ALL RIGHT, WHAT'S GOING ON HERE? BEAT IT, YOU TWO! SCRAM!

...INDEED, ONE MIGHT SAY THIS IS WHERE THE FUTURE OF FRANCE LIES.

WORK, FAMILY, COUNTRY...

UN PETIT FRANÇAIS REGARDE BIEN EN FACE

NO SCHOOL THIS AFTERNOON.

REALLY? BUT WE LEFT OUR SCHOOLBAGS—

DON'T WORRY. I'LL GO GET THEM. YOU'RE FREE FOR THE REST OF THE DAY.

BUT BE HOME BEFORE DARK.

I HAVE SOMETHING TO TELL YOU.

C'MON, IT'S GETTING LATE.

HEY! PAPA CLOSED UP SHOP ALREADY!

PAPA?

COME ON UP! I'M IN YOUR ROOM.

UH... WE'RE HOME, PAPA.

YES. SIT DOWN. LET ME TELL YOU A STORY.

FOR ONCE, I'M GOING TO TELL YOU MY STORY.

AS A BOY, I LIVED IN RUSSIA. THE CZAR RULED OVER RUSSIA. HE LIKED MAKING WAR, AND TO DO SO, HE SENT OUT EMISSARIES TO ROUND UP LITTLE BOYS AND MAKE SOLDIERS OF THEM.

NOW, I DIDN'T WANT TO BE A SOLDIER. I KNEW I'D BE MISTREATED. SO WHEN I WAS OLD ENOUGH TO GO, MY FATHER TOOK ME ASIDE...

...AS I'M DOING WITH YOU, TONIGHT.

HE SAID, "YOU DON'T HAVE MUCH CHOICE. YOU MUST LEAVE. YOU'LL GET BY ON YOUR OWN VERY WELL BECAUSE YOU'RE NOT STUPID."

YOUR MOTHER'S STORY IS A BIT LIKE MINE. IT'S QUITE ORDINARY, IN FACT. I MET HER IN PARIS. WE FELL IN LOVE, GOT MARRIED, AND HAD YOU.

I SAID YES . . . I KISSED HIM AND MY SISTERS, AND I LEFT. I WAS SEVEN.

IT WASN'T EASY, BUT I EARNED A LIVING WHILE DODGING THE RUSSIANS. I MET GOOD PEOPLE AND OTHERS WHO WERE BAD. I WALKED A LONG TIME. THREE DAYS IN ONE PLACE, A YEAR IN THE NEXT, AND THEN I CAME HERE, WHERE I'VE BEEN HAPPY.

I SET UP THIS SHOP—QUITE SMALL AT THE START. ANY MONEY I EARNED CAME FROM MY OWN HANDS.

DO YOU KNOW WHY I'M TELLING YOU ALL THIS?

YES. BECAUSE WE'RE GOING TO GO AWAY TOO.

YES, MY SONS. YOU'RE GOING TO GO AWAY. TODAY IT'S YOUR TURN.

YOU CAN'T COME HOME EVERY DAY LOOKING LIKE THIS. I KNOW YOU CAN DEFEND YOURSELF . . .

BUT WHEN YOU'RE OUTNUMBERED, THE BRAVEST THING TO DO IS SWALLOW YOUR PRIDE AND RUN AWAY.

AND THE GERMANS ARE WORSE THAN THE RUSSIANS. TODAY, A YELLOW STAR, TOMORROW COME THE ARRESTS. WE HAVE TO RUN.

WHAT ABOUT YOU AND MAMA?

DON'T WORRY. THE RUSSIANS DIDN'T GET ME AT SEVEN. THE NAZIS WON'T GET ME AT FIFTY.

YOUR BROTHERS HAVE ALREADY MADE IT TO THE FREE ZONE. YOU'LL LEAVE TONIGHT. MAMA AND I STILL HAVE A FEW THINGS TO TAKE CARE OF, AND THEN WE'LL GO TOO.

NOW, REMEMBER WHAT I'M TELLING YOU: TONIGHT, TAKE THE METRO TO THE GARE D'AUSTERLITZ. THERE, YOU'LL BUY A TICKET TO DAX.

RIGHT BY DAX IS A VILLAGE CALLED HAGETMAU. LOOK FOR A PASSEUR THERE. THEY'LL TAKE PEOPLE LIKE YOU, PEOPLE WITHOUT PAPERS, OVER THE LINE.

ONCE YOU'RE ON THE OTHER SIDE, YOU'RE IN UNOCCUPIED FRANCE. YOU'LL BE SAFE.

YOUR BROTHERS ARE IN MENTON, BY THE ITALIAN BORDER. YOU'LL FIND THEM THERE. WE'RE GIVING YOU EACH 5,000 FRANCS.

5,000 FRANCS!

YOU'LL NEED EVERY CENT.

THERE'S ONE MORE THING YOU HAVE TO KNOW. YOU'RE JEWS, BUT YOU MUST NEVER *EVER* ADMIT IT. YOU HEAR? *NEVER!*

COME HERE, JOSEPH.

ARE YOU A JEW?

NO.

DON'T LIE! ARE YOU A **JEW**, JOSEPH?

ALL RIGHT THEN. I THINK I'VE TOLD YOU EVERYTHING.

NO!

PAPA?

YES, JOSEPH?

WHAT IS... A JEW?

WELL, IT'S KIND OF EMBARRASSING, BUT... I DON'T REALLY KNOW.

ALL RIGHT, THEN...

LONG AGO, WE LIVED IN ONE COUNTRY. WE WERE DRIVEN FROM IT AND SORT OF SCATTERED ALL OVER THE WORLD.

EVERY SO OFTEN, WE ARE DRIVEN OUT AGAIN. AND SO WE HAVE TO GO AWAY AND HIDE.

UNTIL THEY GET TIRED OF HUNTING US DOWN.

DONG DONG

WELL, YOU'RE ALL SET. IN YOUR KNAPSACK YOU'LL FIND MONEY AND AN ADDRESS FOR HENRI AND ALBERT.

SAY GOOD-BYE TO YOUR MOTHER AND GO.

AU REVOIR, MAURICE.

AU REVOIR, JO. SEE YOU SOON.

AW, C'MON! YOU'D THINK THEY WERE NEWBORNS LEAVING THE NEST FOR GOOD! GO ON NOW. SEE YOU SOON, BOYS!

OVER HERE! HURRY!

IT'S LONGER THIS WAY BUT LESS CROWDED.

AND NOW, TIME TO SPOT THE NICEST GUY CLOSE TO THE FRONT.

MONSIEUR, MY LITTLE BROTHER ... HE'S GOT A BAD FOOT. WE COME FROM FAR AWAY ... COULD YOU ...?

GO AHEAD, KIDS. MY TRAIN WON'T ARRIVE FOR A WHILE.

TWO FOR DAX ONE-WAY, THIRD CLASS.

Saint Jean	20ᴴ08
urne	21ᴴ05 - 23ᴴ0
via Dax	21ᴴ10 - 22ᴴ2
ngoulême	21ᴴ
des	22ᴴ
au	23ᴴ

TRACK 7. WE'VE STILL GOT HALF AN HOUR. LET'S TRY AND FIND SEATS.

OH, NO!

LOOK AT ALL THESE PEOPLE! HOW ARE WE GOING TO GET ON BOARD?

Quai 2 Voie 7

RÉSERVÉ* SOLDATS ALLEMANDS

LET'S GET ON HERE.

WHAT A MESS! CAN I HAVE MY SANDWICH?

YEAH, BUT YOU BETTER HIDE IT, OR YOU'LL MAKE EVERYONE JEALOUS.

THIS IS IT! LOOK, WE'RE MOVING!

* RESERVED FOR GERMAN SOLDIERS

GOING FAR, CHILDREN?

TO DAX.

AND YOU'RE TRAVELING ALONE? DON'T YOU HAVE PARENTS?

YEAH, THEY'RE . . .

THEY'RE MEETING US THERE. THEY'RE SICK. I MEAN, OUR MOM IS.

WHAT ARE YOUR NAMES?

JOSEPH MARTIN. AND HE'S MAURICE MARTIN.

WELL, JOSEPH AND MAURICE, I BET YOU'RE THIRSTY AFTER THOSE SANDWICHES!

OUI, MADAME.

HAVE SOME LEMON SODA.

BUT JUST A LITTLE. THIS BOTTLE HAS TO LAST THE WHOLE RIDE!

26

SKREEEE

DAX! LAST STOP!

LOTS OF PEOPLE JUMPED OFF WHEN THE TRAIN SLOWED DOWN.

C'MON. LET'S WAIT INSIDE THE COMPARTMENT.

HALT!

HALT!

PAPERS.

PAPERS.

FATHER, WE DON'T HAVE ANY PAPERS.

IF YOU LOOK SCARED, THE GERMANS WILL NOTICE THAT WITHOUT YOUR TELLING THEM. COME HERE, CHILDREN.

PAPERS.

* THANK YOU.

IS THAT REALLY YOU?

YES. I'VE LOST SOME WEIGHT, BUT THAT'S ME.

AH, THE WAR, THE RATIONING...BUT PRIESTS DON'T EAT MUCH.

THAT'S NOT TRUE AT ALL, AT LEAST IN MY CASE.

OH, THE CHILDREN ARE WITH ME.

HA HA! FINE. BUT DON'T LET YOURSELF GO, FATHER. PEOPLE NEED YOU!

WE CAN GET OFF NOW. WHERE ARE YOU HEADED?

HAGETMAU. FROM THERE WE'LL TRY TO CROSS THE LINE.

GOOD. LET'S HAVE SOME BREAKFAST AT THE STATION, AND THEN I'LL TAKE YOU TO THE BUS.

HERE WE ARE. YOU CAN BUY TICKETS AT THE COUNTER OVER THERE. IT'S TIME FOR ME TO SAY GOOD-BYE.

WAIT! MAURICE AND I WANT TO THANK YOU FOR WHAT YOU DID.

WHAT DID I DO?

YOU LIED TO SAVE US. YOU SAID WE WERE WITH YOU.

I DIDN'T LIE. YOU WERE WITH ME, JUST LIKE ALL THE CHILDREN IN THE WORLD. THAT'S EVEN ONE OF THE REASONS I'M A PRIEST: TO BE WITH THEM.

GO ON NOW. HURRY. SOMETIMES IN LIFE YOU NEED TO.

FATHER, WHAT DID THEY DO TO THE OLD LADY?

THEY DIDN'T DO A THING. SINCE SHE DIDN'T HAVE PAPERS, THEY SENT HER BACK HOME.

BUT YOU'LL MAKE IT ACROSS.

YES, FATHER . . .

. . . WE WILL.

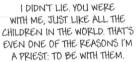

35

CRIPES, IT SURE IS DEAD AROUND HERE!

DONG

DONG DONG

OH, RIGHT. NOON! EVERYBODY'S EATING LUNCH.

UH . . .

WE COULD STOP FOR A BITE TOO, RIGHT?

YOU'RE RIGHT, LET'S GO. DON'T WANT TO DIE OF HUNGER.

SHUT THE DOOR, KIDS! WE'RE NOT TRYING TO HEAT THE SIDEWALK! WHAT DO YOU WANT?

WE WANT LUNCH!

THEN RIGHT THIS WAY! THERE'S A TABLE IN THE BACK!

WE'VE GOT LENTILS WITH BACON AND STUFFED EGGPLANT. CHEESE OR FRUIT FOR DESSERT AND RADISHES WITH SALT FOR STARTERS. THAT OK?

GREAT, THANKS!

WE'RE GOING TO RUN INTO EVERYONE FROM RUE MARCADET HERE. THEY'RE ALL PEOPLE LIKE US: JEWS ON THE RUN.

EAT YOUR DESSERT. LET'S NOT HANG AROUND.

GOOD THING WE'RE NOT STAYING IN THIS TOWN. WITH WHAT THEY SERVE, WE'D TURN INTO SKELETONS! MY RADISHES WERE HOLLOW, AND I'M STILL LOOKING FOR THE BACON IN THOSE LENTILS.

DON'T WORRY, WE'LL TRY CROSSING TONIGHT. IT SHOULD BE LESS DANGEROUS IN THE DARK.

BUT FIRST WE HAVE TO FIND A PASSEUR.

BONJOUR, MADAME HUDOT! HERE'S YOUR ORDER!

MERCI, MADAME HUDOT! AU REVOIR, MADAME HUDOT! SEE YOU NEXT TIME!

WELL, LOOKY HERE.

HEY! HOW 'BOUT SOME INFORMATION?

?!

I'LL TELL YOU BEFORE YOU EVEN ASK. LOOKING FOR A PASSEUR?

UH . . . YEAH.

PIECE OF CAKE! LEAVE TOWN ON THE MAIN ROAD, AND FIRST FARM ON YOUR RIGHT, ASK FOR OLD BEDARD. 5,000 FRANCS A PERSON.

5,000 FRANCS!

THERE'S ANOTHER WAY. RAYMOND WILL TAKE YOU FOR JUST 500 SMACKERS. RAYMOND, THAT'S ME.

BUT YOU HAVE TO FINISH MY MEAT DELIVERIES FOR ME. THE ADDRESSES ARE ON THE PACKAGES, AND YOU HAVE TO COLLECT TIPS. HOW'S THAT SOUND?

34

IT SOUNDED GOOD.

MEET UP AT TEN TONIGHT!

UNDER THE BRIDGE BY THE ARCH! CAN'T MISS IT. THERE'S ONLY ONE!

DO WE HAVE ENOUGH MONEY?

SURE, WE HAVE IT! BUT WE'LL BE BROKE AFTER THAT.

EH, DOESN'T MATTER. ONCE WE'RE IN THE FREE ZONE, WE'LL MANAGE. JUST THINK! IF WE HADN'T MET THAT GUY, AT 5,000 A HEAD, WE'D BE STUCK!

MEANWHILE, WE'VE GOT MEAT TO DELIVER!

PSST!

39

DON'T BE FRIGHTENED. I...I WON'T HURT YOU.

YOU FROM AROUND HERE?

NO.

ARE YOU JEWISH?

NO.

I AM. MY WIFE AND HER MOTHER ARE IN THE WOODS. I'M TRYING TO GET ACROSS.

WHAT HAPPENED TO YOU?

A PASSEUR DITCHED US IN THE WOODS IN THE MIDDLE OF THE NIGHT ABOUT TWENTY MILES FROM HERE. I FELL DOWN TRYING TO GRAB HIM. HE TOOK 20,000 FRANCS. WE'VE BEEN WALKING EVER SINCE.

LOOK, WE'RE TRYING TO CROSS TOO. MEET US AT TEN UNDER THE BRIDGE AT THE OTHER END OF TOWN. YOU CAN ASK OUR GUIDE IF HE'LL TAKE YOU TOO.

THANK YOU! THANK YOU WITH ALL MY HEART! WE'RE SO TIRED...

I HOPE IT WORKS. SEE YOU TONIGHT! THANK YOU, THANK YOU!

CRACK

OOPS!

DON'T WORRY, LI'L BUDDY! NO NEED TO BE JUMPY. JUST FOLLOW ME, DO WHAT I DO, AND DON'T WORRY ABOUT THE REST!

UH . . . RAYMOND? I THINK THERE'S SOMEONE ON OUR RIGHT.

YEAH, A DOZEN SOMEONES. WE'LL LET THEM GET AHEAD OF US AND THEN FOLLOW. WE CAN SIT DOWN FOR A MOMENT.

IS IT STILL FAR?

IF WE WENT STRAIGHT, WE'D BE THERE IN A JIFFY. BUT WE HAVE TO CIRCLE THE CLEARING.

OK, WE'RE CLEAR. LET'S GO!

NOW, FOLLOW THIS TRAIL. IN MAYBE TWO HUNDRED YARDS, YOU'LL REACH A DITCH. WATCH OUT, IT'S DEEP AND FULL OF WATER. PAST THAT, YOU'LL FIND A FARMHOUSE.

PERFECT! THIS WAY, EVERYONE!

GO ON IN, EVEN IF IT'S DARK. THE FARMER KNOWS WHAT'S GOING ON. YOU CAN SLEEP IN THE HAY, AND YOU WON'T BE COLD.

YOU MEAN . . . THAT'S THE FREE ZONE OVER THERE?

THE FREE ZONE?

HA, YOU'RE IN IT ALREADY!

BUT... IS IT USUALLY THIS EASY? I THOUGHT THERE'D BE WATCHTOWERS, BARBED WIRE, PATROLS WITH DOGS...

YOU ALMOST SOUND DISAPPOINTED! NO, IT'S NOTHING LIKE THAT. USUALLY IT GOES REAL SMOOTH. THE GUARD POSTS ARE FAR APART, AND THE ONLY DANGER'S FROM PATROLS.

BUT THEY HAVE TO GO BY THE FORD NEAR THE BADIN FARM, AND WHEN HE SEES THEM, THE OLD MAN SENDS HIS SON TO WARN US.

NOW DON'T GO THINKING IT'S THIS EASY ALL OVER. LESS THAN FIFTEEN MILES FROM HERE, SOME PEOPLE WERE KILLED RECENTLY. IT'S GETTING HARDER ALL THE TIME.

AU REVOIR! AND SAFE TRAVELS!

THIS IS THE PLACE, BOYS.

?!

THERE'S STRAW IN THE SHED AND BLANKETS BEHIND THE DOOR.

SLEEP AS LONG AS YOU WANT.

YOU NEED ANYTHING, JUST KNOCK ON THE LITTLE WINDOW BEHIND THE HENHOUSE. SEE IT? THAT'S WHERE I SLEEP. GO ON. GOOD NIGHT.

GOT IT. THANKS! GOOD NIGHT, MONSIEUR!

45

MAURICE?!

OH, SORRY! EXCUSE ME!

?!

MAURICE?! WHERE WERE YOU?

* I'LL BE BACK. DON'T SAY ANYTHING TO ANYONE.

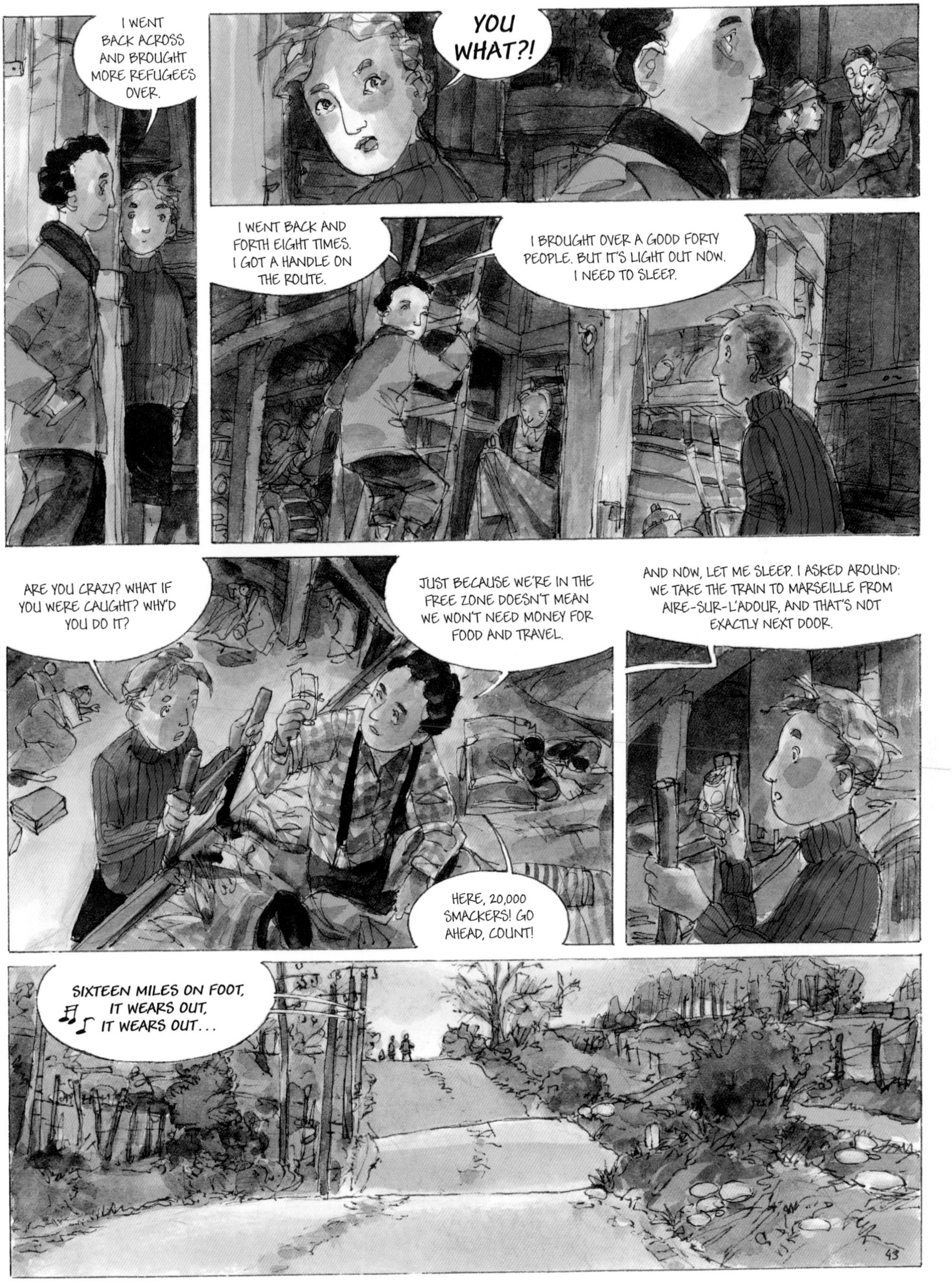
I WENT BACK ACROSS AND BROUGHT MORE REFUGEES OVER.
YOU WHAT?!
I WENT BACK AND FORTH EIGHT TIMES. I GOT A HANDLE ON THE ROUTE.
I BROUGHT OVER A GOOD FORTY PEOPLE. BUT IT'S LIGHT OUT NOW. I NEED TO SLEEP.
ARE YOU CRAZY? WHAT IF YOU WERE CAUGHT? WHY'D YOU DO IT?
JUST BECAUSE WE'RE IN THE FREE ZONE DOESN'T MEAN WE WON'T NEED MONEY FOR FOOD AND TRAVEL.
HERE, 20,000 SMACKERS! GO AHEAD, COUNT!
AND NOW, LET ME SLEEP. I ASKED AROUND: WE TAKE THE TRAIN TO MARSEILLE FROM AIRE-SUR-L'ADOUR, AND THAT'S NOT EXACTLY NEXT DOOR.
SIXTEEN MILES ON FOOT, IT WEARS OUT, IT WEARS OUT...
43

WHOA!

PARDON ME, MONSIEUR. WOULD YOU BE GOING TO AIRE-SUR-L'ADOUR BY ANY CHANCE?

AS A MATTER OF FACT, I AM. TO BE PRECISE, I'M GOING WITHIN A MILE OF THERE.

UM . . .

WOULD YOU . . . I MEAN, COULD ME AND MY BROTHER RIDE IN YOUR BUGGY?

MY DEAR FELLOW, THIS IS NO BUGGY. IT'S A BAROUCHE!

OH . . . SORRY.

KNOW THIS: YOU'RE NEVER TOO YOUNG TO LEARN TO CALL THINGS BY THEIR PROPER NAMES. BUT IT DOESN'T MATTER. YOU MAY RIDE WITH ME.

?!

THANKS, MONSIEUR!

CRIMINY! WHERE'D YOU FIND THIS GUY?

46

AS YOU CAN SEE, OUR SPEED IS LIMITED AND THE COMFORT RUDIMENTARY. BUT IT'S STILL BETTER THAN WALKING. MY CAR WAS REQUISITIONED FOR SOME OFFICER IN THE OCCUPIED ZONE.

AS FOR THIS OLD HORSE, IF I MAY CALL HIM THAT, HE'S THE LAST I HAVE LEFT. I MUST SAY, HIS DAYS ARE NUMBERED. I WON'T BE ABLE TO HARNESS HIM MUCH LONGER.

ALLOW ME TO INTRODUCE MYSELF: I AM THE COUNT DE V.

YOU SEE, CHILDREN, WHEN A COUNTRY LOSES A WAR SO CLEARLY AND DECISIVELY, IT'S BECAUSE THE LEADERS FAILED TO MEASURE UP.

LET ME MAKE IT PLAIN: THE REPUBLIC FAILED TO MEASURE UP!

FRANCE WAS ONLY GREAT WHEN THE KINGS WERE IN POWER! UNDER THE MONARCHY, NEVER WOULD WE HAVE SUBMITTED TO COLONIZATION FROM WITHIN BY ALL KINDS OF FOREIGN ELEMENTS WHO'VE BROUGHT THE COUNTRY TO THE BRINK OF THE ABYSS . . .

WHAT FRANCE LACKED WAS A GREAT REACTIONARY NATIONAL MOVEMENT, WHICH WOULD HAVE ENABLED HER TO RECOVER HER STRENGTH AND FAITH. THAT'S WHAT WE NEEDED TO DRIVE THE HUN BACK ACROSS THE BORDER!

THESE WORDS *LIBERTÉ, ÉGALITÉ, FRATERNITÉ* CRADLED THE PEOPLE IN FALSE HOPE, MASKING THE TRUE VALUES OF THE FRENCH SPIRIT: GRANDEUR, SACRIFICE, ORDER, PURITY . . .

YOUNG MEN, YOU HAVE LISTENED TO ME POLITELY AND ATTENTIVELY.

I HAVE NO DOUBT MY WORDS WILL SOON TAKE ROOT IN YOUR YOUNG MINDS. AND SO, TO THANK YOU AND CONGRATULATE YOU, I SHALL TAKE YOU ALL THE WAY TO THE STATION.

NO THANKS ARE NECESSARY.

DAMN . . .

MARSEILLE,
HERE WE COME!

HEY, MAURICE!
LOOK!

TICKETS
ARE PRETTY
CHEAP . . .

48

SO LET'S HIT THE STREETS AND COME BACK LATER!

WE HAVE SOME TIME TO KILL. THE TRAIN FOR MENTON'S NOT TILL TONIGHT. BUT THE FIRST SHOW'S NOT TILL TEN.

WHOA!

SHIT.

THE SEA...

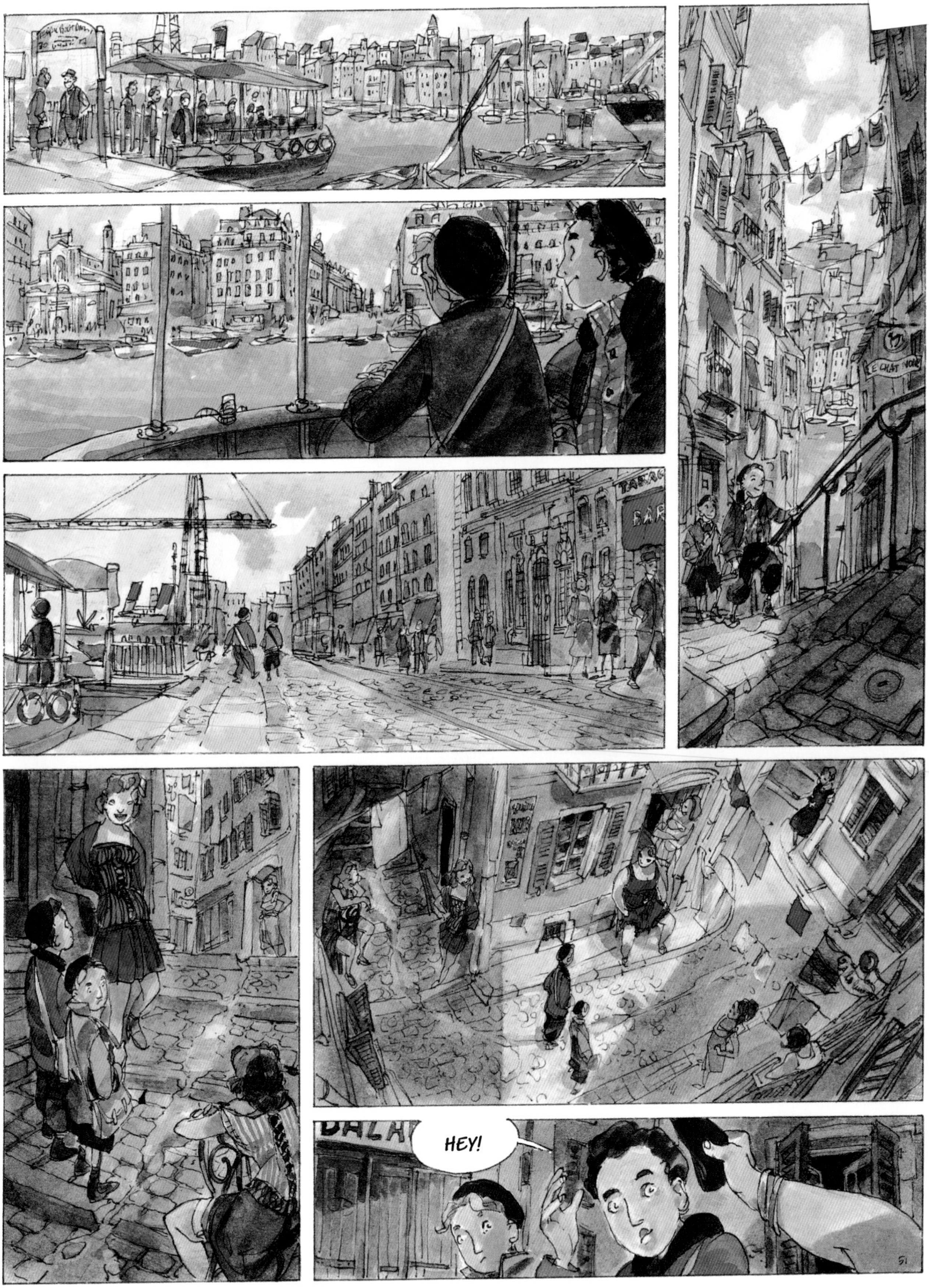
HEY!
LE CHAT NOIR
TABAC
BAR

THERE'S STILL PLENTY OF TIME BEFORE WE LEAVE. WHAT SHOULD WE DO?

THE SAME FILM THREE TIMES IN A ROW, THAT WAS A BIT MUCH! AND IT'S FOUR O'CLOCK ALREADY.

YEAH, BUT IT WAS GREAT! NOW MY TUMMY IS GROWLING AND I HAVE A HEADACHE. HOW ABOUT A PASTRY?

WE COULD GO LOOK AT THE SEA AGAIN. FOR A WHILE.

THAT'S AFRICA OVER THERE.

OVER THERE, BY ITALY.

HOW 'BOUT MENTON? WHERE'S THAT?

FINDING OUR BROTHERS SHOULD BE EASY. I HAVE THEIR ADDRESS, AND THERE CAN'T BE THAT MANY BARBERSHOPS.

?

'SCUSE ME.

HEY! YOU! WHERE ARE YOU GOING?

JUST HEADING TO THE TRAIN.

WE FIGURED THAT. WHERE ARE YOUR PAPERS?

UH... MY DAD HAS THEM.

WHERE'S HE?

54

OVER THERE. TAKING CARE OF THE LUGGAGE.

WHERE DO YOU LIVE?

HERE IN MARSEILLE.

WHAT'S YOUR ADDRESS?

WE'RE ON CANEBIÈRE, OVER THE MOVIE THEATER.

MY DAD OWNS THE MOVIE THEATER.

YOU GO THERE A LOT?

YEAH! I SEE EVERY NEW MOVIE. RIGHT NOW IT'S BARON MUNCHAUSEN. IT'S GREAT!

ALL RIGHT. GET GOING.

MERCI! AU REVOIR, MESSIEURS!

?!

BONJOUR, MONSIEUR! DO YOU HAVE THE TIME?

?!

CAN'T YOU READ A CLOCK?

OF COURSE I CAN!

THEN JUST LOOK UP! THERE'S A CLOCK THAT'LL TELL YOU JUST AS WELL AS I CAN!

OH, RIGHT! THANKS, MONSIEUR!

?!

THEY'RE GONE. C'MON.

WE JOINED IN THE STAMPEDE AND CHARGED TO THE FRONT.

FOR A MINUTE, IT WAS TOTAL CHAOS. THE FEW TRAINS COMING THROUGH WERE ALL OVERBOOKED.

BUT LUCK WAS WITH US. THE TICKET INSPECTORS HADN'T LOCKED THE DOORS, AND WE CLIMBED IN.

AFTER MORE THAN HALF AN HOUR'S DELAY, THE TRAIN LURCHED TO LIFE, AND WE LET OUT A HUGE SIGH OF RELIEF. WE WERE ON THE LAST LEG OF OUR JOURNEY.

58

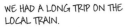
WE HAD A LONG TRIP ON THE LOCAL TRAIN.

IT OFTEN STOPPED IN THE MIDDLE OF NOWHERE. WORKERS WALKED ON THE TRACKS, AND HALF-ASLEEP, I HEARD THEIR VOICES, THEIR ACCENTS, THEIR CURSES.

DAWN BROKE NEAR CANNES, AND SOON AFTER, THE TRAIN ARRIVED IN MENTON.

I DON'T REALLY KNOW HOW...

...BUT I FOUND MYSELF IN A SQUARE WITH PALM TREES WAVING THEIR FRONDS ABOVE MY HEAD.

THEY WERE THE FIRST I'D EVER SEEN.

END OF PART ONE

60

part two

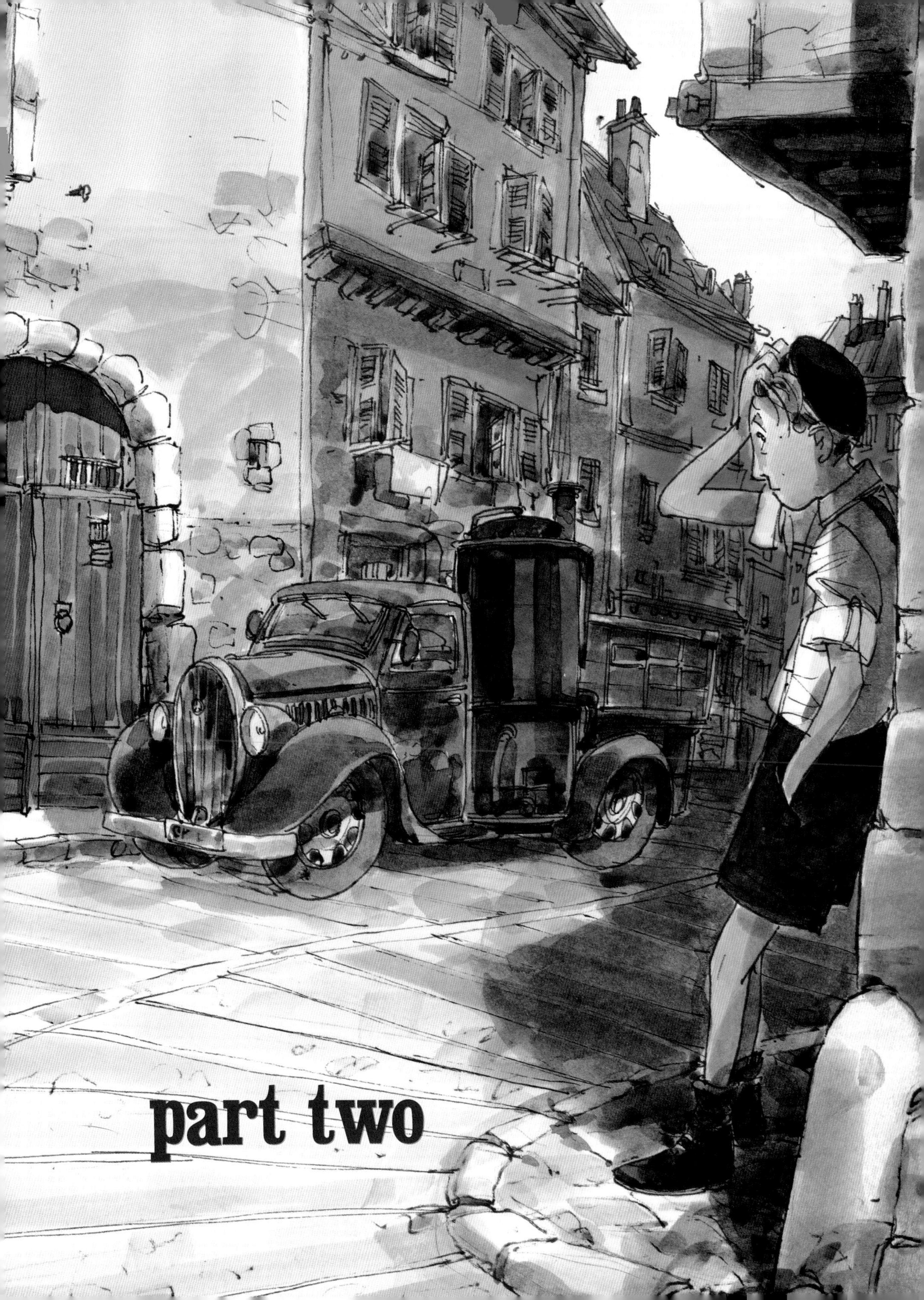

WE'VE BEEN IN MENTON FOR TWO WEEKS NOW.

RIGHT FROM THE START, THIS LITTLE TOWN, RINGED BY MOUNTAINS PLUNGING INTO THE MEDITERRANEAN, HAD CAST A SPELL OVER ME, WITH ITS ARCADES, ITS OLD CHURCHES, AND FLIGHTS OF STAIRS.

ITALIAN OCCUPATION TROOPS COULD ALWAYS BE FOUND LAZING AROUND TOWN.

OUR BIG BROTHERS HAD DONE WELL FOR THEMSELVES, TO SAY THE LEAST.

THEY WORKED AT A BARBERSHOP AND EARNED A GOOD LIVING.

THEY RENTED A LITTLE APARTMENT IN THE OLD TOWN, OVERLOOKING THE SEA.

...ENDLESS GAMES OF SOCCER ON THE BEACH, AND BOUNDLESS WANDERING ALONG STREETS AND PATHWAYS.

FROM THOSE EARLY DAYS, I REMEMBER MEALS THAT SEEMED MASSIVE AND MOUTHWATERING...

PRECIOUS FREEDOM: WE'D FOUND IT AT LAST.

WE WERE USED TO DEPENDING ON OURSELVES AND SOON FOUND JOBS. MAURICE WORKED AT A BAKERY AND CAME BACK WITH HIS HAIR AND EYEBROWS GRAY FROM FLOUR.

I WATCHED OVER COWS ON A MOUNTAIN FARM. I STAYED UP THERE FOR TEN DAYS BEFORE HEADING BACK TO TOWN, LADEN WITH BACON AND EGGS.

IT WAS A MONDAY, WHEN EVERYTHING WAS USUALLY CLOSED. I WAS SURE TO FIND MY BROTHERS SLEEPING IN, AND MY MOUTH WAS ALREADY WATERING AT THE THOUGHT OF THE GIANT OMELET THAT WOULD BEDECK OUR BREAKFAST.

UP AND AT 'EM, CITY SLICKERS! YOUR COUNTRY BROTHER'S HERE, AND HE ISN'T EMPTY-HANDED!

?!

WHAT'S THE MATTER?

WHY THE LONG FACES?

WE GOT SOME BAD NEWS.

MAMA AND PAPA?

MIGHT AS WELL TELL YOU UP FRONT. THEY WERE ARRESTED.

HOW DID IT HAPPEN?

THEY LEFT PARIS AFTER A MASSIVE ROUNDUP AND MADE IT TO THE FREE ZONE, BUT THE VICHY AUTHORITIES CAUGHT THEM THERE AND PUT THEM IN A CAMP.

THEY MANAGED TO GET THIS LETTER THROUGH. THAT'S HOW WE FOUND OUT.

... LOCKED UP IN A CAMP. IF YOU MEET UP WITH THE LITTLE HOOLIGANS, PUT THEM IN SCHOOL. IT'S VERY IMPORTANT. I'M COUNTING ON YOU. I KISS YOU ALL. BE BRAVE. PAPA AND MAMA

WELL, I GUESS I'M GOING THERE.

SO WHAT DO WE DO NOW?

BUT IF YOU GO, THEY'LL KNOW YOU'RE JEWISH! THEY'LL LOCK YOU UP TOO!

THAT'S WHAT I SAID YESTERDAY TOO. BUT WE'VE BEEN UP ALL NIGHT TALKING AND WE FINALLY AGREED ON ONE THING: WE HAVE TO TRY SOMETHING.

I'LL BE BACK AS SOON AS I CAN. ALBERT WILL ENROLL YOU IN SCHOOL THIS AFTERNOON. WORKING IS ALL WELL AND GOOD, BUT PAPA'S RIGHT.

SCHOOL IS VERY IMPORTANT, RIGHT?

RIGHT...

4

REALLY, IT'S QUITE BOTHERSOME, NOT HAVING THEIR PAPERS. IN THEORY, I'M NOT ALLOWED TO LET THEM ENROLL.

BUT WE CAN'T VERY WELL DEPRIVE THEM OF AN EDUCATION, CAN WE?

SO IT'S SETTLED, THEN! I'LL SHOW THEM TO THEIR CLASSROOMS.

RIGHT NOW?

OF COURSE. WHEN ELSE?

IF YOU PLEASE, SIR, I'LL BRING THEM BACK TOMORROW MORNING. THEY STILL NEED SATCHELS AND NOTEBOOKS.

TRUE, TRUE. AND DON'T FORGET SLATES AND CHALK. THOSE WILL BE USEFUL. THE SCHOOL WILL SUPPLY THE BOOKS.

"DAWN," BY ARTHUR RIMBAUD. "I HAVE KISSED THE SUMMER DAWN. BEFORE THE PALACES, NOTHING MOVED."

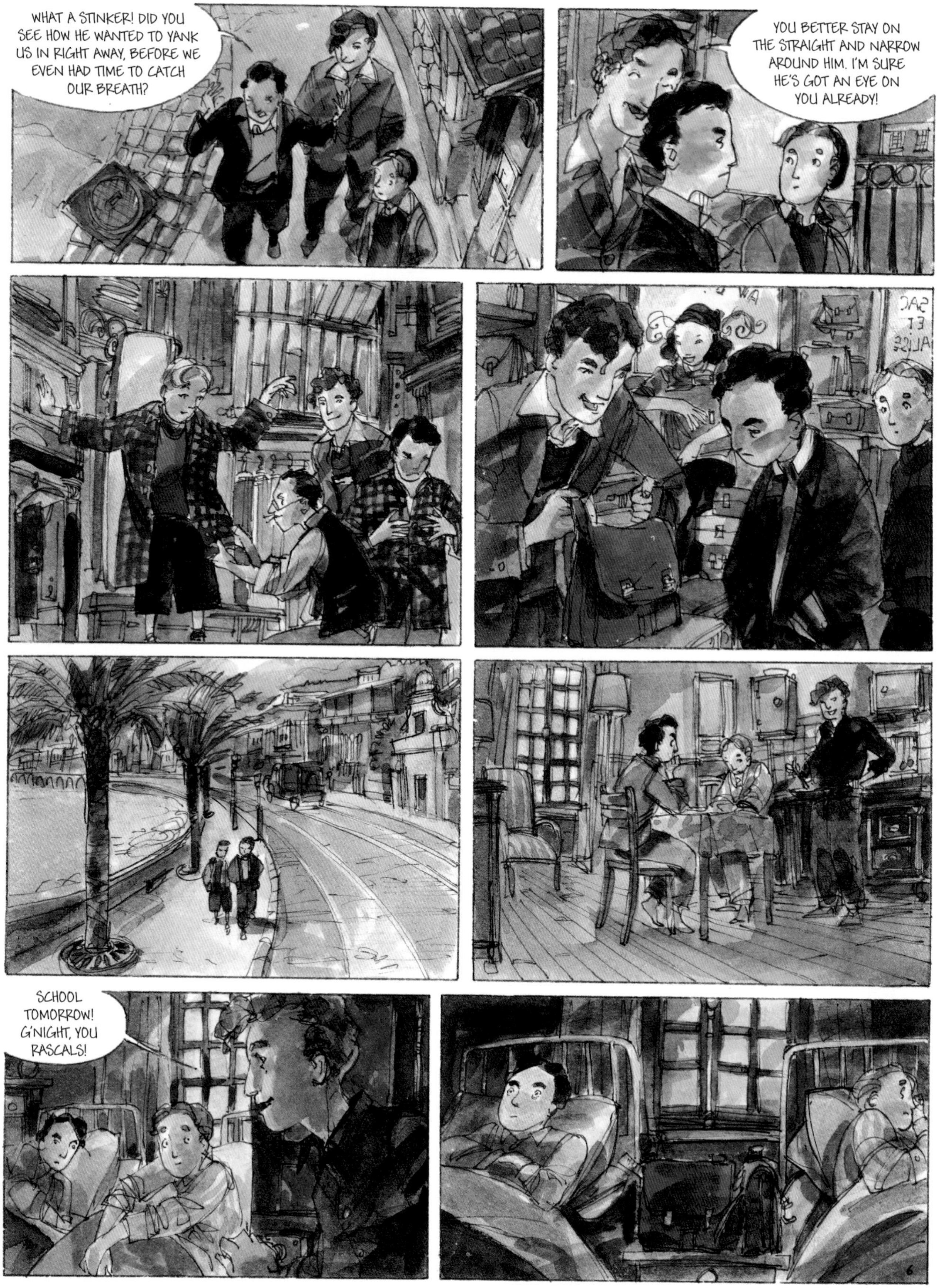
WHAT A STINKER! DID YOU SEE HOW HE WANTED TO YANK US IN RIGHT AWAY, BEFORE WE EVEN HAD TIME TO CATCH OUR BREATH?
YOU BETTER STAY ON THE STRAIGHT AND NARROW AROUND HIM. I'M SURE HE'S GOT AN EYE ON YOU ALREADY!
SCHOOL TOMORROW! G'NIGHT, YOU RASCALS!

?!

CLIC

MAMA AND PAPA ARE FREE.

WE LISTENED AS HENRI TOLD HIS TALE, HANGING ON HIS EVERY WORD. IT WAS WORTHY OF THE HEROIC EXPLOITS OF GRANDFATHER JOFFO.

AT THE CAMP IN PAU, HENRI GOT OFF ON THE WRONG FOOT.

BUT THERE'S BEEN A MISTAKE! SERGEANT, I SWEAR MY PARENTS AREN'T JEWS!

THERE MUST BE SOME WAY WE CAN REACH AN UNDERSTANDING!

YOU HAVE TO GET IN AND SEE THE COMMANDANT. BUT I'M TELLING YOU . . .

UNLESS YOU HAVE CONNECTIONS, HE WON'T SEE YOU.

OF COURSE. BUT WE'RE ORDINARY PEOPLE. WE'VE NEVER BEEN INVOLVED IN POLITICS. MY FATHER WAS JUST COMING TO HELP ME OUT AT THE BARBERSHOP WHERE I WORK.

YOU'RE A BARBER? SAY, MAYBE WE CAN WORK SOMETHING OUT AFTER ALL!

COULD YOU GIVE ME A LITTLE TRIM? I DON'T HAVE TIME TO GO INTO PAU, AND THE CAPTAIN'S REAL HARD ON LONG HAIR.

I COULD GET MY LEAVE REVOKED.

I'LL SEE WHAT I CAN DO ABOUT YOUR PARENTS. NO PROMISES, EH?

AND SO WITH A RAZOR BORROWED FROM THE OWNER AND WATER FROM THE COFFEEMAKER, HENRI GAVE HIM THE BEST HAIRCUT OF HIS LIFE.

THEN HENRI SPENT THE NIGHT WAITING IN A ROOM OF A FLEABAG HOTEL.

THE NEXT MORNING, HE SHOWED UP AT THE SENTRY BOX.

MICHAUD. SERGEANT MICHAUD. HE TOLD ME TO COME HERE AT TEN O'CLOCK.

I DON'T WANT TO HEAR IT! CIVILIANS AREN'T ALLOWED TO LOITER OUTSIDE THE GATES. BEAT IT!

BONNART! IT'S OK! LET HIM IN. I'LL TAKE CARE OF IT.

SORRY, BUT WE HAVE TO BE REAL STRICT WITH SECURITY.

I UNDERSTAND . . .

HE'LL SEE YOU ALL RIGHT, BUT BE CAREFUL. HE'S GROUCHY TODAY.

HE USUALLY IS, BUT TODAY HE'S EVEN WORSE. HERE WE ARE. GOOD LUCK.

OFFICE

THANK YOU SO MUCH, SERGEANT.

KNOCK KNOCK

COME IN!

SIT DOWN.

MONSIEUR COMMANDANT, I'M FRENCH. I WAS AT DUNKIRK AND THE BELGIAN CAMPAIGN.

I'M NOT HERE TO BEG FAVORS BUT TO TELL YOU THERE'S BEEN A MISTAKE. NO ONE IN MY FAMILY IS JEWISH.

HENRI JOFFO. MAKE IT SHORT. IN COMING HERE, YOU'RE RISKING YOUR FREEDOM WITHOUT ANY GUARANTEE OF FREEING YOUR PARENTS.

WE'RE UNDER ORDERS TO HAND OVER ALL FOREIGN JEWS TO THE OCCUPATION AUTHORITIES.

NOW, I'VE GOT 600 SUSPECTS HERE. IF I LET EVEN ONE GO WITHOUT A VALID REASON, I MIGHT AS WELL RELEASE THE REST.

WHAT PROOF DO YOU HAVE?

FIRST OF ALL, MY MOTHER'S CATHOLIC. YOU HAVE HER FAMILY REGISTER. HER MAIDEN NAME IS MARKOFF. I CHALLENGE ANYONE TO FIND A SINGLE JEW NAMED MARKOFF.

IN FACT, WE'RE DESCENDED FROM THE JUNIOR BRANCH OF THE ROMANOFFS—THE RUSSIAN ROYAL FAMILY.

THERE'S NO WAY A MEMBER OF THE ROYAL FAMILY COULD HAVE BEEN JEWISH. THAT WOULD'VE BROUGHT THE RUSSIAN ORTHODOX CHURCH TUMBLING DOWN!

AND YOUR FATHER?

ALL JEWS WERE STRIPPED OF THEIR CITIZENSHIP BY THE GERMANS. BUT AS HIS PAPERS ATTEST, MY FATHER'S FRENCH.

IF HE'S FRENCH, HE'S NOT JEWISH. THERE'S NO IN-BETWEEN.

IF YOU WANT TO BE ABSOLUTELY SURE, YOU CAN CALL THE PREFECTURE IN PARIS.

GET ME POLICE HEADQUARTERS IN PARIS. IDENTITY VERIFICATION DEPARTMENT.

HELLO, IDENTITY VERIFICATION DEPARTMENT?

I NEED SOME INFORMATION ABOUT SOMEONE NAMED JOFFO RESIDING ON THE RUE CLIGNANCOURT. PROFESSION: BARBER. HAS HE BEEN STRIPPED OF FRENCH CITIZENSHIP?

THAT'S RIGHT, JOFFO. 12 RUE CLIGNANCOURT.

FINE, THANKS. VERY GOOD.

YOUR FATHER IS IN FACT STILL A FRENCH CITIZEN. I'LL HAVE HIM FREED, ALONG WITH YOUR MOTHER.

HALF AN HOUR LATER, THE THREE OF THEM WERE REUNITED. THEY HOPPED ON THE FIRST BUS TO GET AWAY AS QUICKLY AS THEY COULD.

BUT WHERE ARE THEY NOW?

IN NICE. WE'LL GO SEE THEM ONCE THEY'RE SAFELY SETTLED IN.

HOW COME THE GUY AT THE PREFECTURE SAID OUR PARENTS WEREN'T JEWISH?

WHO KNOWS? MAYBE THE PAPERWORK HADN'T GONE THROUGH YET. A DELAY, AN OVERSIGHT. IT HAPPENS. OR MAYBE THE GUY JUST SAID WHATEVER HE FELT LIKE BECAUSE HE COULDN'T FIND THE FILE.

OR MAYBE THE COMMANDANT LIED.

MAYBE HE FOUND OUT PAPA WAS JEWISH BUT PRETENDED NOT TO SO HE COULD FREE THEM!

I DON'T KNOW. HE SEEMED REALLY STRICT, BUT...

IT COULD BE. YOU NEVER REALLY KNOW.

YES, A HERO WHO HID HIS GENEROSITY UNDER A STERN MASK. THAT WAS BETTER THAN SOME PENCIL PUSHER'S OVERSIGHT. I WAS SURE THAT WAS HOW MY PARENTS WERE SAVED.

SINCE THEN, I'VE COME TO THINK OTHERWISE.

I SEE.

EVERYBODY'S BEING TAKEN, YOU KNOW. WE JUST BRING THE ORDERS. WE DON'T WRITE THEM.

SURE. OF COURSE, OF COURSE.

THAT'S ALL. DON'T FORGET: YOU HAVE TWO DAYS.

GOT IT. AU REVOIR!

WHAT'S THE CWS?

COMPULSORY WORK SERVICE. IT MEANS WE HAVE TO GO TO GERMANY AND CUT KRAUT HAIR. AT LEAST THAT'S WHAT THEY THINK.

YEAH, NO WAY WE'RE WALKING RIGHT INTO THE LION'S DEN! SO THAT'S IT, THEN—WE'RE LEAVING.

WHEN?

TOMORROW MORNING. WE PACK AS FAST AS WE CAN AND LEAVE AT DAWN. NO POINT HANGING AROUND.

WHERE WILL WE GO?

YOU'LL LIKE THIS, JO: WE'RE GOING TO NICE!

IN NICE IT WAS SUMMER...

MARCELLO! MARCELLO!

HELLO, BAMBINO!

THIS WAY, WE'LL GO TO TITO'S.

THERE YOU GO, FELLAS!

BUONGIORNO!

HELLO, JO!

THE TOMATOES, GIVE THEM.

THANKS, MARCELLO! EIGHT POUNDS A BAG IS HEAVY!

A LITTLE LESS OLIVE OIL FOR US AND A LITTLE MORE FOR FRANCE!

YOU GET THIS MUCH EVERY DAY?

WE GET IT BY THE LITER! AND THAT'S NOT COUNTING CANNED FOOD: TUNA IN OIL, SARDINES IN OIL . . .

BUT NEVER ANYTHING FRESH LIKE THESE TOMATOES! WHAT WE NEED TO GO WITH THEM ARE SOME FRESH GREEN HERBS . . .

PARSLEY?

THAT'S IT! PARSLEY!

THE BUTCHER BY THE DOCKS SHOULD HAVE SOME. HE'S A SMOKER.

WE'LL NEED SOME CIGARETTES.

SO THE TRUCK FARMER GIVES US TOMATOES AND SOME CASH FOR ITALIAN OLIVE OIL. WITH THE CASH AND PACKS OF CIGARETTES CARLO SLIPS US, WE CAN BUY BLACK-MARKET RICE.

MAYBE WE COULD HAGGLE DOWN THE PRICE OF RICE AND KEEP A FEW CIGARETTES TO GET PARSLEY FROM THE BUTCHER.

WITH THE RICE, WE CAN GET SACKS OF FLOUR FOR MAMA ROSSO, WHICH THE ITALIANS USE TO MAKE PASTA.

WE GET SOME, PLUS THE MONEY FROM THE TOMATOES, AND VOILÀ!

CARLO, CAN I HAVE TWO PACKS OF CIGARETTES?

YES, I MUST GET THEM. FOUR O'CLOCK?

OK! THEN WE'LL GET YOU SOME PARSLEY!

BACK AT THE BARRACKS, MARCELLO HAS A FRIEND WHO HAS REAL COFFEE TOO. BUT WHAT HE NEEDS IS SHAVING CREAM.

KNOW WHERE TO GET SOME?

HMM . . . I THINK THE HARDWARE STORE ON THE RUE GARIBALDI HAS SOME. YOU KNOW, THE GUY WHO SOLD US A FEW POUNDS OF LENTILS.

I'LL GO. YOU TAKE CARE OF THE PARSLEY?

SURE. MEET BACK AT THE HOUSE?

OK. YOU KNOW WHAT WOULD SAVE US A LOT OF TIME? A BIKE.

OH, SURE! WE MAKE GOOD MONEY, BUT THAT'S A PIPE DREAM.

IT'S NO PIPE DREAM! AT THIS RATE, WE'LL HAVE A BIKE SOON, I'M TELLING YOU!

AND IF THE WAR KEEPS UP, WE'LL EARN ENOUGH TO BUY THE HOTEL NEGRESCO!

HA HA! GO AHEAD!

I'LL BUY MYSELF THE MAJESTIC! WHEN OUR BROTHERS CUT HAIR THERE, THEY'LL HAVE TO GIVE US A PERCENTAGE!

HA HA! OK, SEE YOU LATER!

YOOHOO!

UH . . . SORRY I'M LATE, MAMAN.

?

OH, IT'S YOU, JO.

GO WASH YOUR HANDS BEFORE DINNER. WHERE'S MAURICE?

HE WON'T BE LONG. HE WENT TO THE HARDWARE STORE FOR SOME SHAVING CREAM.

YOU TWO AND YOUR SCHEMES!

SPEAK OF THE DEVIL!

DON'T FORGET, WE'RE LIVING IN AN OCCUPIED COUNTRY.

THOSE ITALIANS MIGHT BE NICE, BUT THE DAY MAY COME WHEN—

AH, WE KNOW ALL THE ITALIANS!

HAVEN'T YOU HEARD? THESE TWO ARE GOING TO BUY THE HOTEL NEGRESCO! THE FUNNY PART IS, SOMETIMES I WONDER IF THEY WON'T ACTUALLY SUCCEED!

HURRY UP AND EAT, JO. NO TIME TO HANG AROUND.

WHERE TO NOW?

WELL, THE HARDWARE STORE'S OUT OF SHAVING CREAM. BUT HE CAN GET SOME MORE BY RESOLING LEATHER SHOES. SO WE HAVE TO SEE THE COBBLER ON RUE SAINT-PIERRE AND TRADE—

SPEAKING OF COBBLERS, LET ME TELL YOU A STORY.

ONE MAN SAYS TO ANOTHER: THERE'S A VERY EASY WAY FOR ALL MEN TO LIVE TOGETHER IN PEACE. JUST KILL ALL THE JEWS AND THE COBBLERS.

THE OTHER LOOKS AT HIM IN ASTONISHMENT. AFTER A MOMENT OF REFLECTION, HE ASKS: WHY KILL THE COBBLERS?

THAT'S EXACTLY THE QUESTION THAT FAILED TO SPRING TO THE MAN'S MIND.

BUT... WHY THE JEWS?

AND THAT'S WHY IT'S A FUNNY STORY.

YES, IN NICE IT WAS SUMMER, AND THE WAR DEFINITELY FELT FAR AWAY.

NOW, STUDENTS, WON'T YOU PLEASE JOIN ME IN THE NATIONAL ANTHEM?

EVERYONE TOGETHER NOW! YOU KNOW THE WORDS!

ONE, TWO, THREE . . .

AUX ARMES, CITOYENS! FORMEZ VOS BATAILLONS! *

MARCHONS! MARCHONS! **

PERFECT! VERY GOOD! IT'S FOUR THIRTY, YOU'RE FREE TO GO.

JOFFO, REMEMBER TO TEAR A PAGE FROM THE CALENDAR TOMORROW, OR I'LL GIVE THE PRIVILEGE TO SOMEONE ELSE!

OUI, MONSIEUR! NO PROBLEM!

8 NOV 1942

SO IT WORKED OUT? YOU GOT HER GIFT?

YEAH, LITTLE BUDDY. A SEAHORSE BROOCH. IT'S GOLDEN, WITH RED GEMSTONES FOR EYES.

BUT IT REALLY MADE A DENT IN OUR SAVINGS, ESPECIALLY SINCE WE'VE HAD TO SLOW DOWN BUSINESS SINCE SCHOOL STARTED.

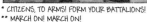

* CITIZENS, TO ARMS! FORM YOUR BATTALIONS!
** MARCH ON! MARCH ON!

THANK YOU, DARLINGS. YOU'VE REALLY OUTDONE YOURSELVES!

IMAGINE THAT—JEWELS FROM THE YOUNGER BOYS, A SEWING MACHINE FROM THE OLDER ONES...

WE NEEDED GIFTS WORTHY OF A ROMANOFF!

NOW, YOUR TURN TO BE SPOILED! I MADE A BUNDT CAKE. IT'S NOT MISSING A SINGLE ALMOND!

YUMMM!

BUT A MOTHER'S BIRTHDAY IS PRICELESS...

I'LL JUST HAVE A BITE. IT'S TIME FOR THE BRITISH BROADCAST.

TELL US THE NEWS! I CAN'T BRING MYSELF TO LEAVE DESSERT!

OK, BUT SAVE ME SOME! I NEVER SAID I'D SACRIFICE IT ON THE ALTAR OF CURRENT EVENTS.

SPEAKING OF WHICH, I HAD A CUSTOMER WHOSE HUSBAND WORKS FOR THE VICHY NEWS SERVICE. SHE CONFIRMED THAT THE KRAUTS TOOK A BEATING IN STALINGRAD!

THEY MIGHT EVEN BE CLOSE TO—

THE ALLIES HAVE LANDED IN NORTH AFRICA! ALGERIA AND MOROCCO!

HAPPY BIRTHDAY, DARLING!

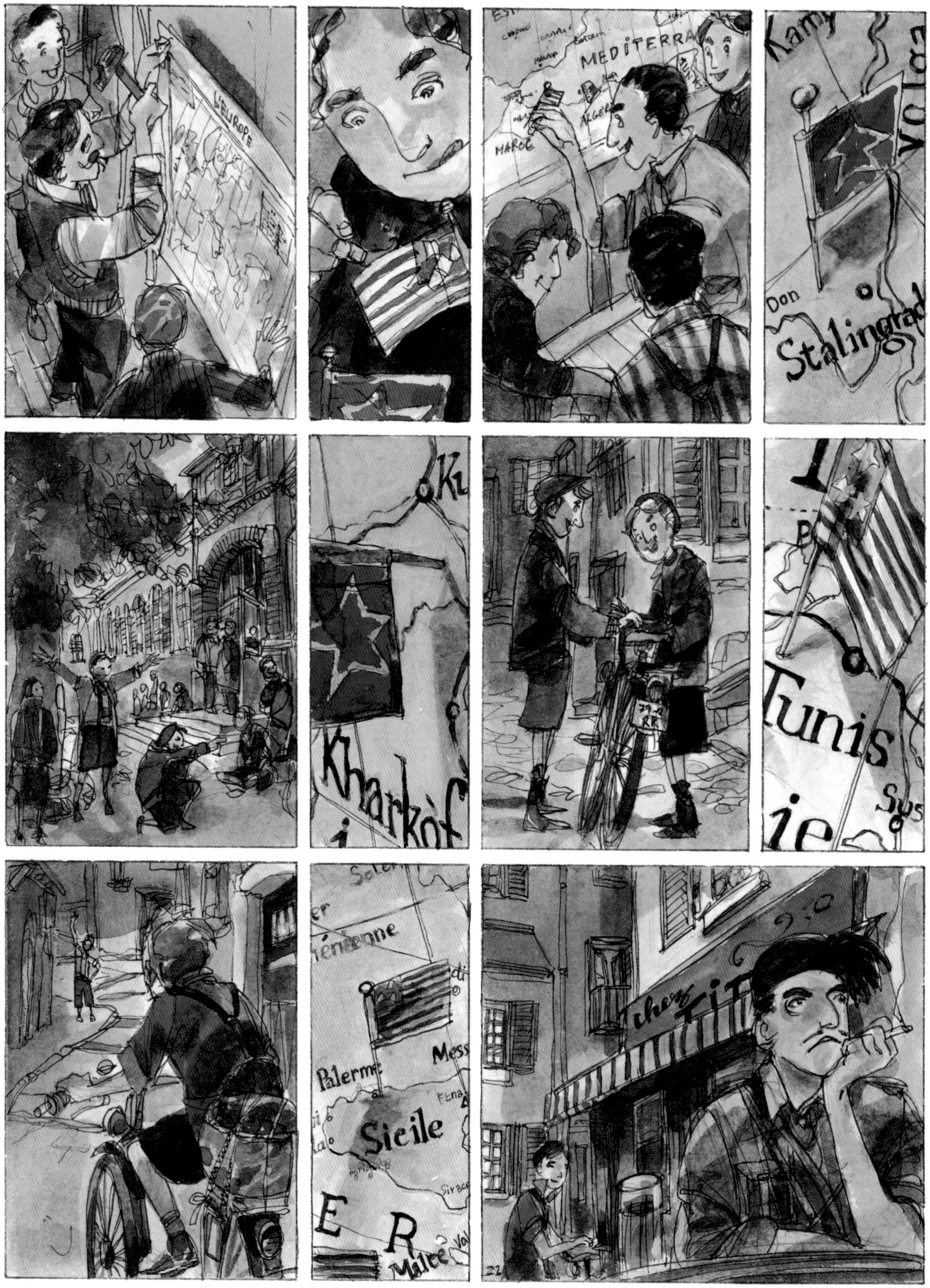
L'EUROPE
MEDITERRA
MAROC
ALGER
Volga
Don
Stalingrad
Kharkof
Tunis
Palerme
Sicile
Etna
Malte
chez

HELLO, MARCELLO! I . . . I'M HERE FOR YOUR FRENCH LESSON.

SALUT, JO! I DIDN'T SEE YOU. SIT DOWN. I'LL BUY YOU A GRENADINE.

BUT DON'T BOTHER WITH THE FRENCH LESSON. I WON'T HAVE TIME ANYMORE.

I HAVE TO LEAVE SOON.

YOUR REGIMENT GOT TRANSFERRED?

NO, WE'RE ALL LEAVING. ALL THE ITALIANS.

MUSSOLINI'S NOT IN CHARGE ANYMORE. BADOGLIO IS, AND HE'S MAKING PEACE WITH THE ALLIES. SO WE'RE GOING HOME, MAYBE EVEN TO WAR WITH HITLER NOW!

BUT IF YOU'RE LEAVING, THEN WE'RE FREE!

NO. IF WE LEAVE, THEN THE GERMANS WILL COME.

SEPTEMBER 10, 1943 NICE TRAIN STATION . . .

DING
DING
DING

DING

DING
DING
DING
DING
DING

DING
DING
DING
DING
DING
DING

WHAT ARE YOUR BROTHERS UP TO? IT'S SIX ALREADY!

AH, THERE YOU ARE! WE WERE STARTING TO GET WORRIED!

24

WELL?

WELL, IT'S SIMPLE. WE HAVE TO LEAVE RIGHT AWAY.

THE GERMANS ARE ARRESTING ALL THE JEWS AND LOCKING THEM UP IN THE HOTEL EXCELSIOR. THEN SPECIAL TRAINS TAKE THEM AWAY AT NIGHT.

IN SHORT, STAYING HERE IS BUYING A ONE-WAY TICKET TO GERMANY.

WELL, CHILDREN, HENRI'S RIGHT. WE'LL HAVE TO SPLIT UP AGAIN.

HENRI AND ALBERT, YOU LEAVE TOMORROW FOR SAVOIE. I HAVE AN ADDRESS IN AIX-LES-BAINS. THEY'LL HIDE YOU.

JO AND MAURICE, YOU'LL LEAVE FOR GOLFE-JUAN. YOU'LL HEAD FOR A VOLUNTEER YOUTH CAMP NAMED MOISSON NOUVELLE.

IN THEORY, IT'S A VICHY ORGANIZATION CALLED COMPAGNONS DE FRANCE, BUT IN PRACTICE, IT'S SOMETHING ELSE. YOU'LL CATCH ON SOON.

AND YOU?

I'VE HAD TIME TO THINK THESE LAST FEW DAYS. WE'LL STICK WITH THE METHOD THAT'S WORKED WELL BEFORE AND GO IN TWOS.

DON'T WORRY ABOUT US. WE'RE OLD HANDS AT THIS. AND NOW, DINNER, EVERYONE! WE HAVE TO SLEEP EARLY TO BE IN SHAPE FOR TOMORROW.

SO ARE WE GOING IN?

WE'RE GOING IN. A VICHY CAMP IS THE LAST PLACE NAZIS WOULD COME LOOKING FOR TWO JEWISH BOYS.

ARE YOU NEW? WHO SENT YOU?

CLAC

UH... WE WANT TO SEE THE DIRECTOR, MONSIEUR SUBINAGUI.

CLAC

FOLLOW ME.

TWO NEW BOYS TO SEE YOU, MONSIEUR DIRECTOR.

THANK YOU, GERARD. LEAVE US.

CLAC

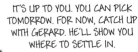

DON'T BE ALARMED. GERARD'S FATHER WAS AN ARMY SERGEANT AND RAISED HIM IN A VERY... SPECIAL ATMOSPHERE.

BUT HE'S QUITE NICE.

YOUR FATHER TOLD ME ABOUT YOU. YOU'LL BE FINE HERE, AND... SAFE.

I'M QUITE BUSY, SO I'LL BE BRIEF. YOU CAN STAY IN CAMP AND SEE TO DAILY OPERATIONS, KITCHEN DUTY, AND CLEANING.

OR YOU CAN WORK AT OUR POTTERY WORKSHOP IN VALLAURIS. OUR COMMUNITY MAKES A LIVING OFF THE PRODUCTS WE SELL. YOU'LL GET WAGES, OF COURSE.

IT'S UP TO YOU. YOU CAN PICK TOMORROW. FOR NOW, CATCH UP WITH GERARD. HE'LL SHOW YOU WHERE TO SETTLE IN.

CLAC

FOLLOW ME!

HERE WE ARE. YOUR BUNKS ARE IN THE BACK.

SUPPER'S AT SIX, WE LOWER THE FLAG AT SEVEN, SHOWER AT EIGHT THIRTY, AND IN YOUR BUNKS BY NINE. LIGHTS OUT AT NINE FIFTEEN.

DON'T WORRY. HE'S A LITTLE CRACKED, BUT HE'S A GOOD GUY.

?

I'M ANGE TESTI. I MANAGED TO DUCK OUT OF KITCHEN DUTY TODAY BY SAYING MY STOMACH HURT.

GOTTA SNEAK A NAP IN, TO GET THROUGH THE DAY.

SO . . . IS IT NICE HERE?

YEAH, IT'S GREAT!

THERE ARE A LOT OF JEWS.

YOU TOO?

UH . . . NO. ARE YOU A JEW?

HA HA! NOT A CHANCE. BAPTIZED, HOLY COMMUNION, CONFIRMATION, AND A CHOIRBOY TO BOOT!

HOW'D YOU WIND UP HERE?

94

WELL, I'M ON VACATION, YOU SEE.

I'LL EXPLAIN. BUT I'M GONNA HIDE DOWN HERE, IF YOU DON'T MIND. IF THE KITCHEN GUY CATCHES ME GOOFING OFF, HE'S NOT GOING TO BE TOO HAPPY!

I'M ORIGINALLY FROM ALGERIA: RIGHT FROM BAB EL-OUED!

I WANTED TO SEE FRANCE. I'D NEVER BEEN BEFORE. MY FATHER SAID OK, SO DURING ALL SAINTS' DAY, I WENT AND STAYED WITH A COUSIN IN PARIS.

THERE I WAS, STROLLING DOWN THE CHAMPS-ÉLYSÉES WHEN THE AMERICANS LANDED IN NORTH AFRICA! NO CHANCE OF GOING HOME BEFORE THE WAR WAS OVER.

Le Petit Parisien

MOISSON NOUVELLE

TO TOP IT ALL OFF, MY COUSIN FOUND A GIRL AND THREW ME OUT! I HEADED SOUTH FOR THE WARM WEATHER, WITHOUT A PENNY TO MY NAME. AFTER A LITTLE PANHANDLING, I WOUND UP HERE. SUBINAGUI AGREED TO TAKE ME IN.

IT'S EASIER THAN SELLING SHOES ALL DAY IN MY FATHER'S SHOP IN ALGERIA.

IMAGINE: IF THE WAR LASTS TEN YEARS, I'LL HAVE HAD A TEN-YEAR VACATION!

HOW MANY KIDS ARE IN THE CAMP?

OH, ABOUT A HUNDRED. SOME COME, SOME GO. IT DOESN'T CHANGE MUCH, BUT IT'S A NICE PLACE. YOU'LL SEE.

CLANG CLANG

AH! SUPPERTIME! NOT A MINUTE TOO SOON!

C'MON, ALL THE GOOD STUFF GETS SNAPPED UP FAST!

APART FROM A FEW
DOWNSIDES HERE AND
THERE, THAT WAS THE START
OF THREE WONDERFUL
WEEKS . . .

MAURICE?

HNNH?

I HEARD SUBINAGUI TALKING TO THE COOK. SOUNDS LIKE THE NAZIS HAVE STEPPED UP THE HUNT FOR JEWS. EVERYONE SUSPECTED OF BEING JEWISH IS BEING SHIPPED STRAIGHT TO GERMAN CAMPS.

I KNOW. AND IF THE KRAUTS RAID THIS PLACE, I THINK THEY'LL KNOW WE'RE JEWISH RIGHT AWAY.

HOW? UP TILL NOW—

THE GESTAPO DOESN'T EVEN BOTHER ASKING ANYMORE. OUR NAME IS JOFFO, AND WE COME FROM THE JEWISH QUARTER IN PARIS? THAT'S ENOUGH FOR THEM!

SO WHERE ARE WE FROM?

ALGIERS.

AND WHAT DID OUR PARENTS DO?

PAPA CUTS HAIR. MAMA DOESN'T WORK.

AND WHERE DO WE LIVE?

10 RUE JEAN-JAURÈS.

SO WE HAVE TO MAKE SOMETHING UP. REMEMBER ANGE'S STORY? WELL, SAME WITH US. WE CAME TO FRANCE ON VACATION AND GOT STUCK BECAUSE OF THE ALLIED LANDING.

THEY WON'T BE ABLE TO CHECK OUT OUR STORY. NO WAY TO CONTACT OUR FRIENDS OR PARENTS.

WHY 10 RUE JEAN-JAURÈS?

BECAUSE THERE'S A RUE JEAN-JAURÈS IN EVERY TOWN, AND 10 IS EASY TO REMEMBER.

IF THEY ASK ABOUT OUR HOUSE OR THE STORE, JUST DESCRIBE RUE CLIGNANCOURT. THAT WAY WE WON'T MESS ANYTHING UP.

C'MON, DON'T WORRY. GET SOME SLEEP. WE'RE NOT ALONE HERE, AND SUBINAGUI WILL HELP US.

COMPAGNONS DE FRANCE

THERE'LL ALWAYS BE SOMEONE TO HELP US.

31

LOOK AT THAT! WE'RE SO LUCKY FERDINAND SAID WE COULD COME ALONG ON HIS GROCERY RUN! NOW WE'LL GET TO SEE OUR PARENTS!

HEY, JOFFOS! THERE'S NICE! HELLOOOO!

YOU GOT ANY PLANS?

NO! WE'RE JUST GOING TO WALK AROUND.

OK. I GOTTA STOP ON RUE DE RUSSIE, SEE A PAL REAL QUICK.

AFTER THAT, I'LL SHOW YOU WHERE THE BUS STATION IS SO YOU DON'T MISS YOUR RIDE HOME TONIGHT.

THEN YOU'RE FREE!

IT'S OVER HERE.

JUST WAIT. I'LL BE BACK IN A MINUTE.

WHAT'S HE UP TO?

HE'S BEEN GONE MAYBE TWO MINUTES.

ARE YOU NUTS? IT'S BEEN AT LEAST TEN!

HOW CAN YOU TELL IT'S BEEN TEN? DO YOU HAVE A WATCH?

I DON'T NEED A WATCH! I CAN TELL. IF YOU CAN'T TELL THE DIFFERENCE BETWEEN TWO MINUTES AND HALF AN HOUR, YOU MIGHT AS WELL JUMP OFF THE NEAREST DOCK.

WHATEVER, STUPID...

WELL I'VE HAD IT. I'M GOING LOOKING FOR HIM. WE CAN FIND THE STATION BY OURSELVES ANYWAY, AND I WON'T SPEND THE WHOLE AFTERNOON COOLING MY HEELS.

JUST WAIT HERE FOR ME. I'LL BE RIGHT BACK.

JEEZ, WHAT ARE THOSE JERKS UP TO?

IF THIS IS SOME TRICK, I'M GONNA . . .

OK, I'M COUNTING MY STEPS TO THE DOOR, AND IF THEY'RE NOT BACK BY THEN, I'M GOING BACK TO CAMP. THEY CAN JUST STUFF IT.

1...2...3...

17...18...19...

33...34...35...

36!

MAURICE?
FERDINAND?

MAURICE?

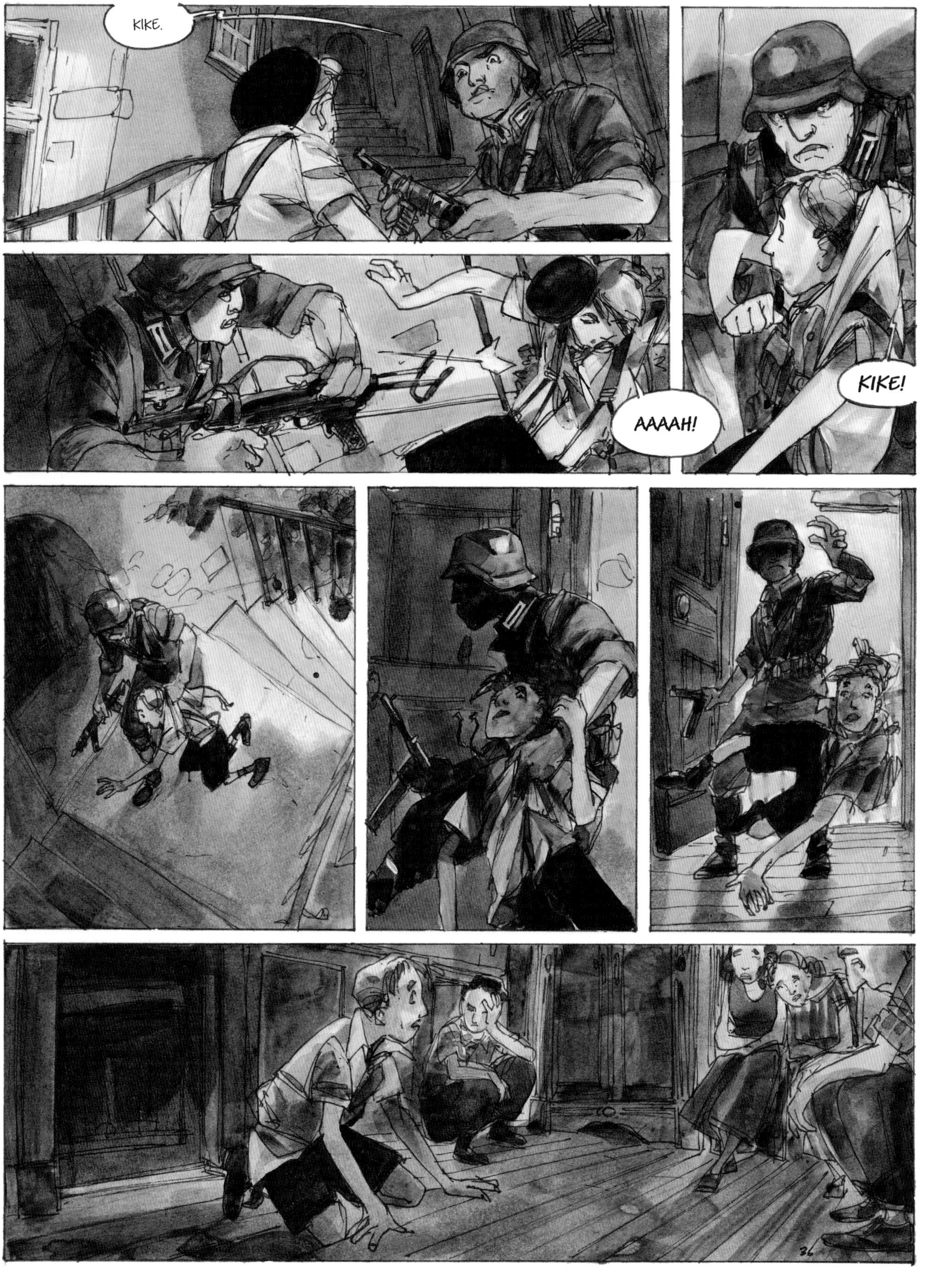
KIKE.
AAAAH!
KIKE!

WHAT'S GOING ON?

IT'S MY FAULT. WE WALKED INTO A TRAP. THERE WAS A RÉSISTANCE CENTER HERE THAT SUPPLIED FAKE PAPERS AND PASSAGE TO SPAIN.

BUT WHY'D YOU COME HERE? WHY DID YOU NEED THAT STUFF?

BECAUSE I'M A JEW.

DON'T WORRY. YOU'LL BE FINE. WHEN THEY FIND OUT YOU'RE NOT JEWS, THEY'LL LET YOU GO.

WE'LL SEE.

WHY ME? I'D GIVE ANYTHING FOR THOSE PAPERS. AND JUST WHEN IT LOOKED LIKE THINGS WOULD BE ALL RIGHT...

POOF...

WHAT TIME IS IT?

QUARTER AFTER FIVE.

ALREADY? WE'VE BEEN HERE FOR MORE THAN THREE HOURS! WHAT ARE THEY DOING?

MAYBE THEY FORGOT US? THEY MUST BE LOOKING FOR THE RÉSISTANCE LEADERS. WE'RE WORTHLESS TO THEM.

I WOULDN'T BET ON IT, BROTHER. BUT ONCE THEY'VE QUESTIONED US, THEY'LL REALIZE THEIR MISTAKE. AT LEAST I HOPE SO . . .

OR ELSE WHAT? THEY'VE NABBED US ALL. WHAT A HAUL! NOW THAT THEY'VE GOT US, THEY'LL PROBABLY GO ON AND WIN THE WAR!

WHAT DID WE EVER DO TO THEM? THAT SOLDIER, THE WAY HE LOOKED AT ME . . . IT WAS LIKE ALL HE'D EVER DREAMED OF WAS SMASHING ME AGAINST THE WALL.

THIS IS RIDICULOUS. I'M ELEVEN YEARS OLD. I DON'T KNOW ANY GERMANS. HOW CAN I BE THEIR ENEMY?

OUTSIDE! SCHNELL! SCHNELL! *

* QUICKLY!

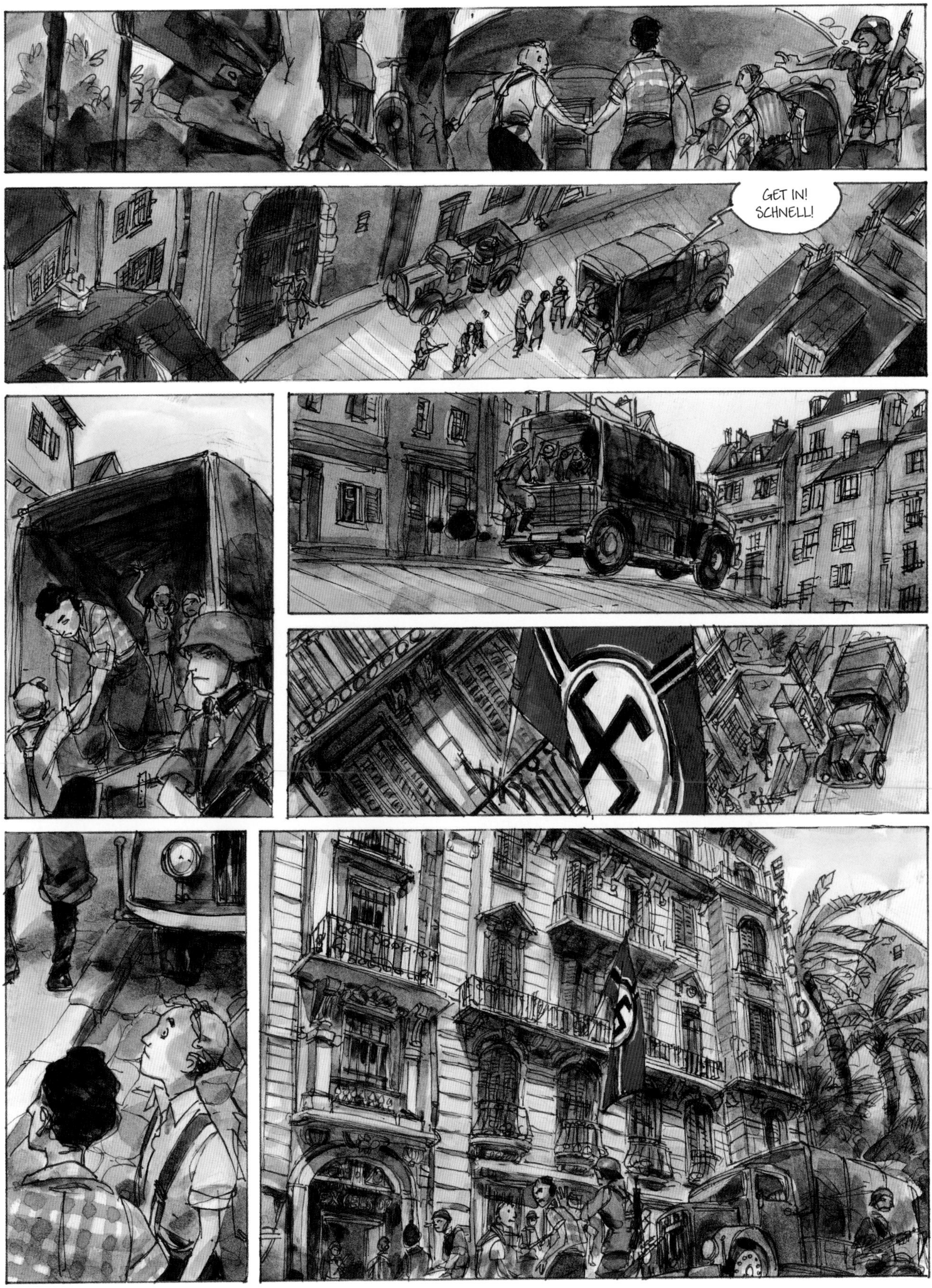
GET IN!
SCHNELL!

JAWOHL! **

ICH BRINGE DIESE DREI HOCH, UM ANZUFANGEN. IHR WARTET HIER MIT DEN KINDERN. ICH GEBE EUCH BESCHEID. *

* I'M BRINGING THESE THREE UPSTAIRS TO START WITH.
YOU GUYS WAIT HERE WITH THE KIDS. I'LL LET YOU KNOW.
** YES, SIR!

* YOU, THERE! IT'S YOUR TURN! BRING THEM UP!.
** GO RIGHT IN, THE BOTH OF YOU!

107

YOUR TURN NOW. YOU ARE BROTHERS?

YES. HE'S JOSEPH, AND I'M MAURICE.

JOSEPH AND MAURICE WHAT?

JOFFO.

...AND YOU'RE JEWS.

NO, WE'RE NOT!

WE'RE NOT JEWS, WE'RE FROM ALGERIA. WE WERE ON VACATION IN FRANCE AND GOT STUCK BECAUSE OF THE LANDING.

WHAT WERE YOU DOING ON RUE DE RUSSIE?

WE CAME FROM THE COMPAGNONS DE FRANCE CAMP. FERDINAND TOOK US ON HIS GROCERY RUN, AND WE WERE WAITING FOR HIM LIKE HE TOLD US TO, WHILE HE WENT TO SEE A FRIEND. NO ONE KNEW HE WAS A JEW.

AND YOU'RE CATHOLIC?

OF COURSE.

YOU'VE BEEN BAPTIZED?

YES, AND WE'VE TAKEN COMMUNION.

WHICH CHURCH?

LA BUFFA, IN NICE.

WHY NOT ALGIERS?

MAMAN LIKED FRANCE BETTER. SHE ALSO HAD A COUSIN AROUND HERE.

VERY WELL, WE WILL VERIFY ALL THIS. FOR NOW, YOU WILL UNDERGO A PHYSICAL EXAMINATION, TO SEE IF YOU'RE CIRCUMCISED.

NO, WE'RE NOT JEWS!

LOOK, JUST IGNORE HIM. HE CAN'T SPEAK FRENCH. YOU CAN TELL ME THE TRUTH. IT WON'T LEAVE THIS OFFICE. YOU'RE JEWS.

NO, OUR PARENTS HAD US OPERATED ON WHEN WE WERE LITTLE BECAUSE WE HAD ADHESIONS, THAT'S ALL.

SO APART FROM THIS, YOU'RE NOT JEWS, RIGHT?

SURE, A PHIMOSIS. EVERYONE WHO COMES THROUGH THAT DOOR SAYS HE HAD A PHIMOSIS AS A KID. WHERE WAS THE OPERATION?

WHAT HOSPITAL?

DUNNO, WE WERE KIDS.

YEAH, MAMAN CAME TO SEE ME. SHE BROUGHT CANDY AND A BOOK.

IT WASN'T A...WHAT YOU SAID. WE GOT OPERATED ON IN ALGERIA. AT THE HOSPITAL.

WHAT BOOK?

ROBIN HOOD. WITH PICTURES.

WELL...BRAVO!

MY NAME IS ROSEN. DO YOU KNOW WHAT IT MEANS WHEN YOUR NAME IS ROSEN?

IT MEANS, QUITE SIMPLY, THAT I'M JEWISH. AND YOU CAN TALK TO ME.

SO YOU'RE JEWISH. BUT WE'RE NOT. THAT'S ALL.

DAS IST CHIRURGISCH GEMACHT WORDEN. *

* THIS WAS PERFORMED FOR SURGICAL REASONS.

WELL.

WE CHECKED, AND THE HEAD OF MOISSON NOUVELLE CONFIRMED EVERY DETAIL OF YOUR STORY.

YOU, THE OLDER ONE—GET OUT OF HERE. YOU HAVE ONE WEEK TO BRING US PROOF THAT YOU'RE NOT JEWISH. WE NEED COMMUNION CERTIFICATES FROM THE PRIEST IN NICE. FIGURE IT OUT.

IF YOU DON'T COME BACK, WE'LL MAKE MINCEMEAT OF YOUR BROTHER.

A GUARD WILL LEAD YOU TO ONE OF THE ROOMS WE'RE USING AS CELLS.

BETTER HURRY.

LISTEN, MAURICE, IF YOU THINK YOU HAVE A CHANCE OF FREEING ME, THEN COME BACK. OTHERWISE, KEEP AWAY AND HIDE.

AT LEAST ONE OF US SHOULD STAY ALIVE.

DON'T WORRY. I'LL BE BACK IN A WEEK.

SALUT.

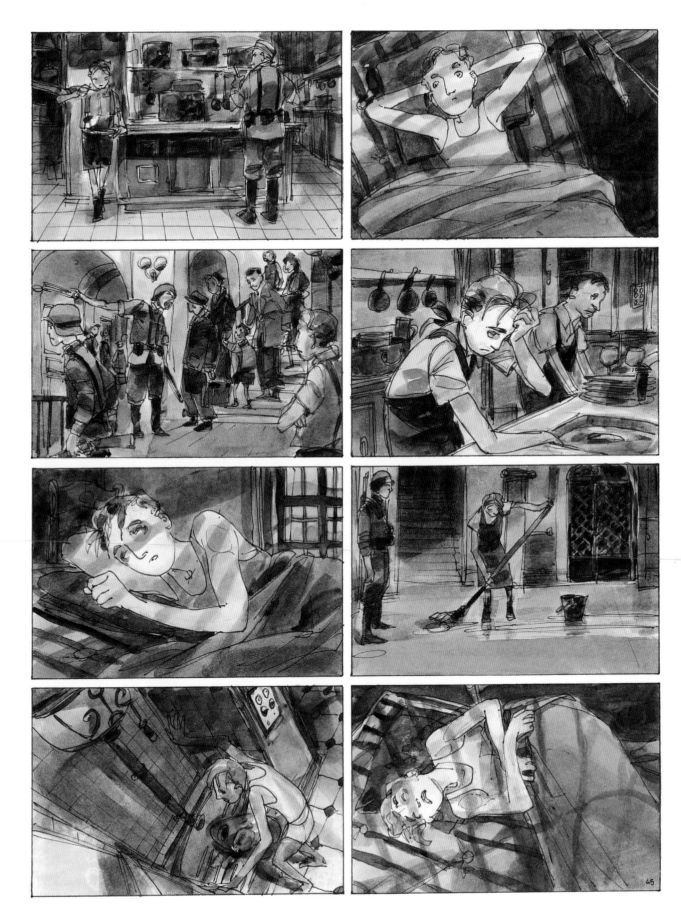

HUH? MAU— MAURICE! YOU'RE BACK!

SO THIS IS WHAT BEING CATHOLIC DOES TO A GUY!

SOUNDS LIKE YOU THOUGHT I WOULDN'T BE!

I GOT THE PAPERS! C'MON GET UP AND GET DRESSED. TODAY WE'RE GETTING OUT OF HERE.

HURRRGH . . . I'M SICK AS A DOG! THE DOCTOR SAYS IT'S THE ONSET OF MENINGITIS! BUT THEY'VE TAKEN GOOD CARE OF ME. HOW'D YOU DO IT?

I WENT TO SEE THE PRIEST IN LA BUFFA. TOLD HIM EVERYTHING AND HE AGREED TO HELP US! HE HAD TO GET THE ARCHBISHOP'S APPROVAL, BUT ARCHBISHOP RÉMOND'S SAVING EVERY JEW HE CAN!

THE PRIEST IS DOWN THE HALL. HE'S BEEN SITTING HERE SINCE SEVEN THIS MORNING TO MAKE SURE THE SS GUYS WILL SEE HIM.

I WENT BACK TO MOISSON NOUVELLE TOO, AND SUBINAGUI'S WAITING OUTSIDE TO TAKE US BACK TO CAMP.

WE HAVE ALL THE PAPERS. ARCHBISHOP RÉMOND EVEN GAVE US BAPTISMAL CERTIFICATES FROM THE CATHEDRAL IN ALGIERS AND A HANDWRITTEN LETTER FROM HIM, THREATENING TO COME IF WE'RE NOT FREED.

VERY WELL. EVERYTHING IS IN ORDER. YOU ARE FREE TO GO.

REALLY, I MUST SAY IT TOOK YOU LONG ENOUGH.

MAURICE, JOSEPH. SAY GOOD-BYE TO THE GENTLEMAN.

AU REVOIR, MONSIEUR!

AU REVOIR, CHILDREN. BE GOOD, GOOD LUCK, AND GOD BLESS!

THANK YOU, FATHER!

AU REVOIR! THANKS AGAIN FOR EVERYTHING!

?

SAY, MONSIEUR SUBINAGUI... WHY ARE OUR BAGS BACK THERE?

WE'RE NOT GOING BACK TO THE CAMP. I'M TAKING YOU STRAIGHT TO THE STATION.

I PUT EVERYTHING YOU NEED IN YOUR KNAPSACKS: CLOTHES, A SNACK, TICKETS... YOU'LL TAKE THE TRAIN TO AIX-LES-BAINS, WHERE YOUR BROTHERS ARE WAITING.

WHAT'S GOING ON?

YOUR FATHER'S BEEN ARRESTED.

IF THE GERMANS TIE HIM TO YOU, THEY'LL COME TAKE YOU BACK. NO SENSE HANGING AROUND. YOU HAVE TO GET GOING RIGHT AWAY.

LUCKILY, YOUR MOTHER WAS WARNED IN TIME AND ESCAPED. I CAN'T SAY WHERE, BUT REST ASSURED, SHE'S SAFE.

I DIDN'T EVEN CRY. A YEAR AGO, I WOULDN'T HAVE BEEN ABLE TO BEAR THE THOUGHT THAT PAPA HAD BEEN ARRESTED. I'VE GROWN, HARDENED, CHANGED...

MY HEART HAS GROWN ACCUSTOMED TO DANGER AND DISASTER. MAYBE I CAN NO LONGER FEEL REAL SORROW. THE LOST CHILD I WAS EIGHTEEN MONTHS AGO WHEN WE LEFT PARIS HAS DWINDLED AWAY BIT BY BIT ON THE TRAINS, THE ROADS OF PROVENCE, THE HOTEL HALLWAYS IN NICE.

THE NAZIS HAVEN'T TAKEN MY LIFE AWAY YET, BUT THEY'VE STOLEN MY CHILDHOOD.

TOMORROW I'LL BE IN AIX-LES-BAINS. IF THAT DOESN'T WORK OUT, WE'LL GO SOMEWHERE ELSE, FARTHER, ANYWHERE. I DON'T CARE. MAYBE I DON'T REALLY CARE THAT MUCH ABOUT LIFE ANYMORE.

BUT THINGS ARE IN MOTION NOW, THE GAME WILL GO ON, AND RULES SAY THE HUNTED MUST ALWAYS RUN FROM THE HUNTER. WHILE I STILL HAVE MY WIND, I'LL DO ALL I CAN TO ROB THEM OF THE PLEASURE OF CATCHING ME.

THROUGH THE WINDOW, I WATCH THE SAD, FLAT FIELDS VANISH BIT BY BIT. IT SEEMS AS THOUGH I CAN ALREADY SEE THE PEAKS, THE SNOW, THE RED AUTUMN LEAVES. ALREADY THE FLOWERS AND FRAGRANCES OF THE MOUNTAINS ARE WASHING OVER ME...

CHRISTMAS 1943, A VILLAGE NEAR AIX-LES-BAINS...

AH, MY DASHING MESSENGER! COME WARM YOURSELF BY THE FIRE, JO. DID YOU DELIVER ALL THE PAPERS?

YES, MONSIEUR MANCELIER. BUT IT'S GETTING HARDER TO BIKE AROUND. THERE'S LOTS OF ICE BEFORE DAWN, AND IT'S SLIPPERY!

YOU HAVE TO GET USED TO IT, MY BOY. A GREAT MAN IS DISTINGUISHED BY HIS ABILITY TO CONQUER THE WORST DIFFICULTIES!

YOU SEE, JOSEPH, THEY DON'T TEACH YOU THAT IN PUBLIC SCHOOL. AND THE SCHOOLS HAVE BECOME PUBLIC, TOO PUBLIC.

50

A GREAT MAN MUST ALSO HAVE IDEALS. AND HE MUST KNOW HOW TO PICK THEM!

IN POLITICS, FOR A MAN WHO'S BORN BETWEEN THE ATLANTIC AND THE URAL MOUNTAINS BUT IS NEITHER A TURK, A NEGRO, OR A COMMUNIST, THERE'S ONLY ONE IDEAL: EUROPE!

A BRIGHT, CLEAN EUROPE CAPABLE OF FENDING OFF ITS ENEMIES FROM THE EAST, WEST, AND SOUTH! HISTORICALLY, NOT MANY HAVE BEEN ABLE TO PULL IT OFF. HOW MANY?

HOW MANY ARE THERE, JOSEPH?

THREE, MONSIEUR MANCELIER.

EXACTLY, JOSEPH. THREE.

LOUIS XIV. NAPOLEON.

PHILIPPE PÉTAIN.

AND THE GREAT MASSES OF MONGRELS AND MORONS HAVE ALWAYS RISEN AGAINST THE GENIUS OF THESE THREE MEN!

PLEASE, AMBROISE! SUCH LANGUAGE!

BUT THIS TIME, WATCH OUT! PÉTAIN'S A TOUGH CUSTOMER. HE WAS AT VERDUN, JUST LIKE ME. AND BELIEVE ME, WHEN YOU'VE BEEN THROUGH VERDUN, YOU CAN GET THROUGH ANYTHING!

WE SHOULD'VE SIDED WITH HITLER AND MUSSOLINI BACK IN '36. NOTHING COULD HAVE STOOD AGAINST US—NOT ENGLAND, NOT RUSSIA! PLUS, WE WOULD'VE AVOIDED SURRENDER IN '40.

HA, HA! EXCEPT THAT IN '36 THE GOVERNMENT WAS ROTTEN TO THE CORE WITH JEWS, WOPS, SOCIALISTS, AND FREEMASONS!

UH . . . FRANÇOISE? WH-WHATCHA DOIN'?

OH, NOTHING. I . . . I WAS JUST, I MEAN . . . I HAVE TO WRITE TO MY FAMILY AND AFTER THAT I—I WAS HEADED TO SEE MY BROTHER MAURICE AT THE HOTEL WHERE HE WORKS.

I'M GOING TO READ A LITTLE. WHY?

NEAT. HAVE FUN, JO!

TH— THANKS.

IF I SCRATCH OUT THIS #4 RATION STAMP . . . IT LOOKS LIKE A #1. NOW WE CAN GET SOME SUGAR! THAT'S THE MOST VALUABLE RATION.

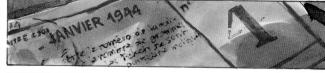

JANVIER 1944

*305 FÉVRIER 1944

MARS 1944

. . . AND SO, DEAR MAMAN, DON'T WORRY. THE MANCELIERS TREAT ME WELL AND ARE STILL TOTALLY IN THE DARK. MAURICE HAS A JOB AS A CLERK AT THE HOTEL DU COMMERCE, AND WE HAVE A FEW SCHEMES ON THE SIDE THAT MAKE LIFE EASIER. NOW THAT YOU'RE WITH OUR BROTHERS IN AIX, WE CAN SEE EACH OTHER SOMETIMES. GIVE THEM A KISS FOR ME. I NEED TO GET BACK TO MY RATION STAMPS NOW.

JE T'AIME, JO

SALUT, JO. HERE TO SEE YOUR BROTHER? HE'S DOWN IN THE CELLAR.

THANKS, I'LL HEAD DOWN!

RiÏÏÏÏÏÏ

?!

LOOK! IT'S THE MILICE! THEY'RE HEADED HERE! *

THEY'RE SURROUNDING THE HOTEL!

?!

KID . . .

FOR MONSIEUR JEAN AT THE CHEVAL-BLANC.

FREEZE! HANDS UP!

* THE FISH IS AN APRIL FOOL'S DAY JOKE.

* THE MILICE FRANÇAISE, OR FRENCH MILITIA, FOUGHT AGAINST THE FRENCH RESISTANCE.

FACE THE COUNTER!

BEAT IT, KID.

WHAT DO YOU WANT WITH MONSIEUR JEAN?

I HAVE A LETTER FOR HIM. BUT IT'S FOR HIS EYES ONLY.

NICE JOB, KID. IF WE NEED YOU AGAIN, WE'LL LET YOU KNOW. FOR NOW, GO HOME.

HOW MUCH FOR YOUR BOOK ON PÉTAIN? THE ONE IN THE WINDOW.

THE BOOK ON THE MARSHAL? ER...FORTY FRANCS.

ALL RIGHT THEN. I'LL BUY IT, BUT I'M NOT TAKING IT. LEAVE IT IN THE WINDOW, IF YOU DON'T MIND.

WITH THIS TAG ON IT, OF COURSE.

WELL...I'D RATHER SET IT ASIDE, IF YOU DON'T MIND.

NEVER MIND, THEN. NO SENSE DROPPING FORTY FRANCS. IN A FEW WEEKS I'LL COME IN AND TAKE WHAT I WANT.

SEE YOU VERY SOON, MONSIEUR MANCELIER.

WELL, MANCELIER? NOT SO CLEVER NOW THAT YOUR MARSHAL CAN'T PROTECT YOU ANYMORE!

LEAVE HIM ALONE! HE HID ME FOR A LONG TIME, AND IT COULD HAVE COST HIM HIS NECK TO HIDE A JEW.

GREAT, SO YOU'RE A JEW. BUT DID THAT OLD FOOL KNOW?

OF COURSE HE DID!

DOESN'T MATTER, HE'S STILL A COLLABORATOR. WE HAD TO TAKE ALL THAT SHIT FROM HIM—

YEAH, BUT MAYBE HE HAD TO ACT THAT WAY TO HIDE JO!

ALL RIGHT, GET UP! WE'LL STASH YOU SOMEWHERE TILL WE FIGURE OUT WHAT TO DO.

I'M GOING. I HAVE LOTS OF PAPERS TO DELIVER!

l'aube

Vive la France!
Vive de Gaulle!

PARIS EST DÉLIVRÉ*

ÉDITION DE 5 HEURES
*PARIS
ACCLAME DE GAULLE
LA GARNISON ALLEMANDE
capitule
après d'âpres combats*

COMBAT
POUR LA RÉSISTANCE À LA RÉVOLUTION

S GESSIER

JOURNAL RÉPUBLICAIN
DU PAYS DE GEX ET DE LA VALLÉE DE LA VALSERINE

*LA LIBÉRATION
du Ht. Bugey, de
la Vallée de
et du Pays de Gex

* PARIS LIBERATED
* PARIS WELCOMES DE GAULLE
* THE GERMAN GARRISON SURRENDERS
* LIBERATION

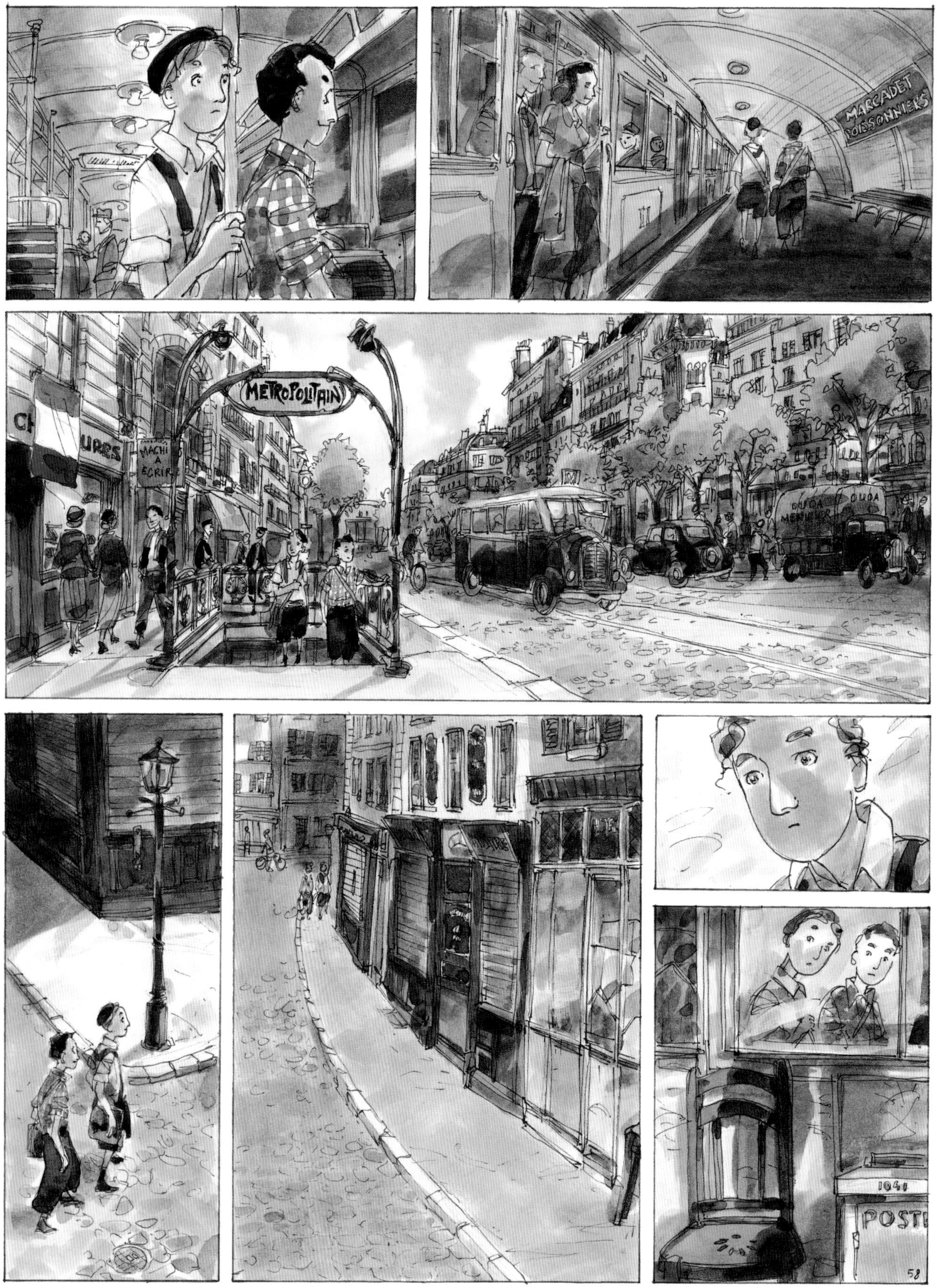
MARCADET POISSONNIERS
METROPOLITAIN
URES
MACHI A ECRIRE
1941
POST

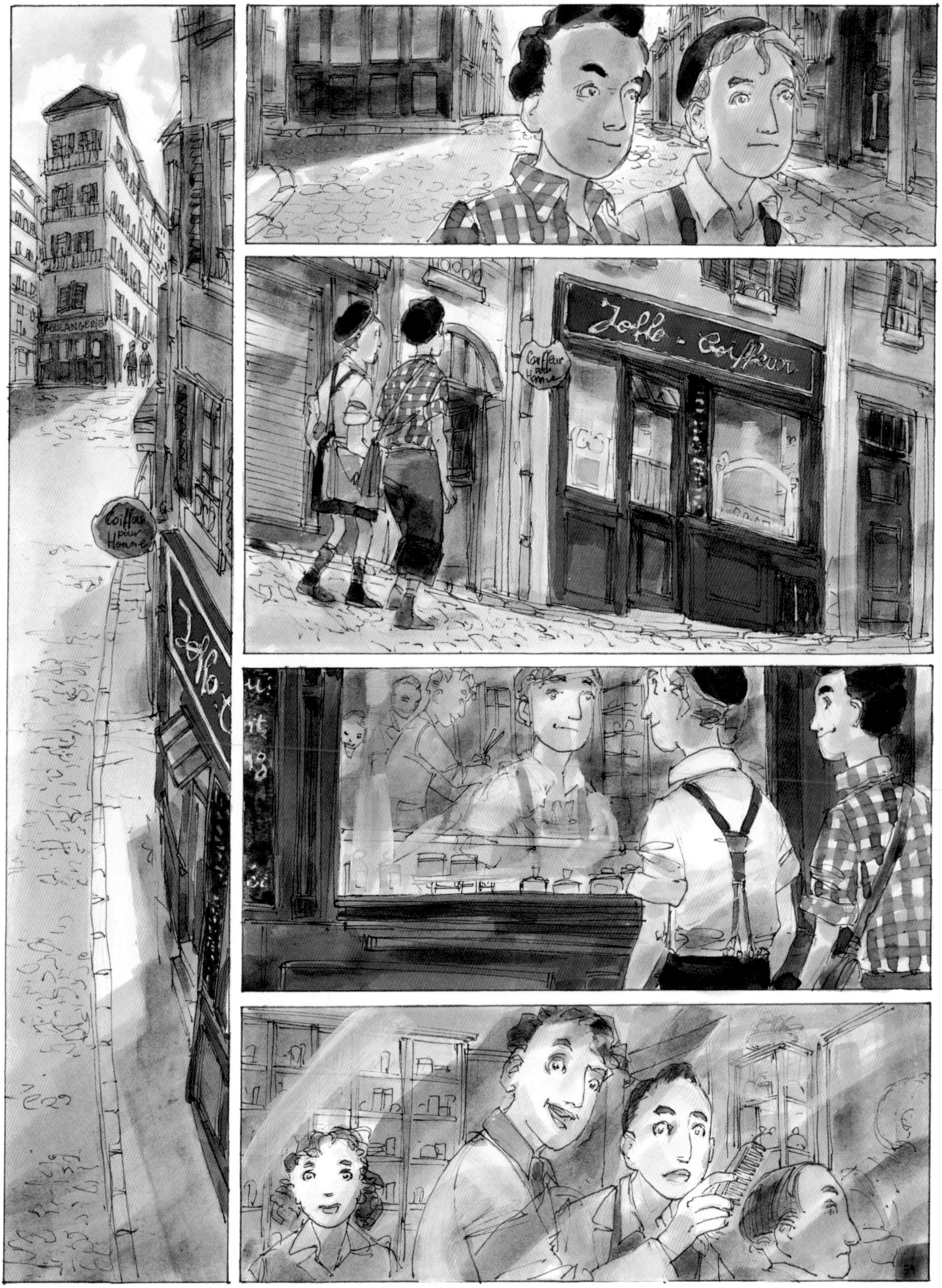
BOULANGERIE
Coiffeur pour Homme
Joffo - Coiffeur
Coiffeur pour Homme

TO ALL THE JOFFO FATHERS

THE END KRIS – BAILLY – JOFFO

Jo and Maurice's Journey, 1941–1944

ENGLAND

NETHERLANDS

GERMANY

ENGLISH CHANNEL

BELGIUM

LUXEMBOURG

Paris

Miles
0   50   100
0   50 100 150
Kilometers

Occupied Zone
(FRANCE)

SWITZERLAND

Ainay-
le-Vieil

Montluçon

ATLANTIC
OCEAN

Free Zone
(FRANCE)

Lyon

Aix-les-
Bains

ITALY

Nice

Hagetmau
Aire-sur-l'Adour

Dax

Menton
Golfe-Juan

Marseille

train
bus/truck
walk/buggy
border between
occupied and
free zones

N

SPAIN

MEDITERRANEAN
SEA

GLOSSARY

au revoir: good-bye, until we meet again (literally, "till seeing again")

bonjour: hello (literally, "good day")

Compagnons de France: Companions of France. A youth group for boys, much like the Boy Scouts

je t'aime: I love you

kike: American slang, a derogatory name for a Jew

kraut: American slang, a derogatory name for a German

liberté, égalité, fraternité: liberty, equality, fraternity. The national motto of France

madame: Mrs., ma'am. A polite title given to a French woman, especially if married

maman: mom, mama

merci: thank you

Milice française: French Militia. A paramilitary force created by the Vichy government to fight against the French Resistance

monsieur: mister, sir. A polite title given to a Frenchman

oui: yes

passeur: a ferryman or smuggler. During World War II, it was a guide who led Jews to the free zone.

la Résistance: the French Resistance

salut: hi, hello. A casual greeting. It can also mean "good-bye".

voilà: there it is (literally, "see there")

FRANCE UNDER GERMAN OCCUPATION

Nine months after the start of World War II, Germany began its invasion of France. In only six weeks, France was defeated. From May 1940 until August 1944, France was occupied by Nazi German forces.

While France was occupied, it was split into two different zones. The occupied zone (in northern France) was governed by Nazi Germany, and people living there were subjected to severe laws. The Nazis enacted strict curfews, and there were extreme food shortages. Countless French citizens were deported to Germany to perform forced labor while thousands of Jewish French citizens were sent to death camps in France and Germany.

The free zone (located in southern France) was ruled by the French government—at that time called the Vichy regime—which operated from a city called Vichy and was led by Philippe Pétain. But the free zone's name was misleading. The Vichy regime collaborated with Germany, and many people living in the free zone were persecuted just as harshly as those living in occupied France. The Vichy regime adopted Nazi legislation from the occupied zone that barred Jews from appearing in various public places, subjected them to curfews, and prevented them from working certain jobs. Homes were raided, and Jews and other minorities were deported or imprisoned. These policies led to the deaths of thousands of French citizens in concentration camps. During this time, a group of French citizens known as the French Resistance secretly rebelled against the German occupation and the Vichy government. Using guerrilla fighting tactics and advanced intelligence, the French Resistance played a vital role in the recapture of France by the Allies. The Allied forces were the countries, including the United States, that were allied against Germany.